Hail Mary

Patti Liszkay

Black Rose Writing | Texas

The author grants the final approval for this literary material.

First printing

This is a work of fiction. Names, characters, businesses, places, events, and
incidents are either the products of the author's imagination or used in a
fictitious manner. Any resemblance to actual persons, living or dead, or
actual events is purely coincidental.

ISBN: 978-1-68433-488-9
PUBLISHED BY BLACK ROSE WRITING
www.blackrosewriting.com

Printed in the United States of America
Suggested Retail Price (SRP) $17.95

Hail Mary is printed in Book Antiqua

*As a planet-friendly publisher, Black Rose Writing does its best to eliminate
unnecessary waste to reduce paper usage and energy costs, while never compromising
the reading experience. As a result, the final word count vs. page count may not meet
common expectations.

Dedicated to my sister, Romaine, one of the most generous, funny, and beautiful people on the planet: I consider myself incredibly lucky to know you, let alone to be related to you.

Special thanks to: Mary Lewis and Carol Metheny, who gave me guidance with the legal aspects of the story; Romaine Rupp for her good advice and input; my children and children-in-law, my most enthusiastic cheering section; and Tom Liszkay, the love of my life.

Hail Mary

Chapter One

All men were snakes. Of this Trysta was one hundred percent sure. They were snakes charmed by a look, a smile, a temptingly served-up sexual invitation, breasts, buttocks, spread legs between which they were helpless to resist slithering. Then they'd slither away without a thought in their stupid male snake-brains about having stuck her with a baby, then two, then three, then four.

And what about the beautiful promises these lying snakes had held out to *her*, tempted *her*, and ultimately seduced *her* with? Love. Security. A future. Happy home, happy life, happy husband, happy wife. Huh, no man better ever again tell her he loved her. Just *see* what it would get him. Trysta sighed sadly. Not that any man actually loved her at the moment. Of this she was also pretty sure.

"Ooooo, Trysta you are so *dumb!*" she muttered to no one, pounding her fists on her knees. There was no one else in the waiting room of this so-called doctor, psychologist, quack, whatever she was, and if Silvio wanted their son Zach to keeping coming here every week, well, let *him* bring him here.

"Right, Trysta, like *that'll* happen," she again muttered to herself, grabbing a copy of *People* from the magazine table to absorb herself in the problems of the rich, beautiful and famous, problems she should be so lucky to have.

***

"Aw, *shit*," Darren muttered, running a hand through his hair and snapping shut his laptop. He'd no sooner gotten the Little Screamers quieted down – that was what he called Trysta's two daughters, but only to himself ever since he once called them that and they liked the title so much that they spent the rest of the day marching around the house shouting "We are the Little Screamers!" punctuating each shout with a scream – and now little...whatever her name was...decides to wake up. How the hell was he supposed to get any work done around here?

"Okay, okay," he said, picking up his four-month-old daughter – or was she his daughter? Well, he'd know soon enough – from the Pack 'n Play on the floor next to his desk.

"Darren," cried nine-year-old Trina, bursting into his office, "Miri's awake!"

"Darren," cried seven-year-old Sam, bursting in behind her sister, "Silvia's awake!"

"I know, I got her," Darren said irritably. "Trina, wouldja grab the changing pad from the diaper bag there and lay it on the desk for me?"

"You're not supposed to call her 'Silvia' anymore," Trina scolded her sister, ignoring her step-father's request, "her name is 'Miri.' Mommy says."

"Hey, come on, somebody grab me the...oh, forget it, I'll get it myself."

"But I like '*Silvia*,'" Sam whined. "Daddy Darren, Trina called you 'Darren.'"

"So did you!" Trina shot back.

"But I only did it because Trina did it! Daddy Darren, Trina sometimes calls you 'Darren.'"

"Tattle-tale!" Trina cried.

"Okay, whatever, stop bickering. Here, somebody take this diaper and throw it into the trash."

"*Ewwww!*" The girls backed away and squealed in high-pitched giggles.

"Daddy Darren," said Sam, sidling up to Darren as he snapped baby Silvia or Miri back into her onesie, "will you still be our daddy when we go back to live with our real daddy?"

"Huh?" asked Darren, stopping in mid-snap. "You're going back to live with your daddy? With Silvio? Wait, is it for sure now?"

"Daddy says *maybe* we will," said Trina, moving next to her sister and close to him. "But Daddy says not to worry because we can see Mommy whenever we want and there will still be lots of people to love us and take care of us, like him, Mommy, our grandmas and grandpas, and maybe we'll go back to our old school."

"Silvio – your dad – he told you that?" Darren felt his heart lifting.

"Can we take Baby Silvia with us when we go live with Daddy?"

"*Sam!*" Trina cried, "I *told* you we're supposed to call her 'Miri!'"

"But Mommy calls her 'Silvia!'"

"But only when she shows her to Daddy when Daddy comes to pick us up."

"What?" asked Darren.

"Mommy says," said Sam, curling a lock of her hair around her finger and imitating her mother's seductive posture and tone of voice, "'Hi-i, Silvio. It's *soooo* good to *see* you. We all miss you so *much!* Little Silvia looks just like you. Want to hold her?'"

"*What?*" asked Darren, nervously bouncing Silvia Miri. "Well...what does Silvio – I mean your dad – say?"

"Oh," said Trina, "he just says, 'No thanks, come on, kids, we gotta go.' Then Daddy looks funny and Zach looks funny 'til we get into the van."

"Daddy Darren," said Sam, "can Silvia come with us when we go live with Daddy? I want her to come live with us."

"Well," said Darren, "we'll just have to see..." *who she belongs to*, he finished in his mind.

After he flushed Trina and Sam out of his office Darren studied the baby in his arms. Blonde hair. Well, that was from Trysta. Brown eyes. Those could be his. Trysta was insisting that this baby, this Miri, Silvia, whatever, was his. Well, *now* she was insisting the baby was his, as she had when she first discovered she was pregnant. Right after the baby was born it was a different story, all right. Trysta was making a bold play for Silvio then – geeze, was she plotting this while she was giving *birth*, for God's sake? He fucking wouldn't put it past her, now that Silvio had come into all that money – but naming the baby, this baby who was supposed to be *his* baby, the baby that he threw away his marriage to Sally for – naming this baby *Silvia*? Was Trysta completely nuts? Or was she just throwing the longest Hail Mary in history?

Darren played over in his mind the events of the past year. It was just a little over a year ago that Trysta announced to him that she was pregnant. With his child. He recalled how at first the words hadn't computed; this was Trysta Jablonski, the sexy receptionist at the high-end real estate management corporation of Highland and Erskerberg where Darren had recently been promoted to Vice-President of Strategic Acquisitions. Trysta was married to a plumber, had three kids, and she and Darren had been having what he thought was a brief celebratory fling, a little treat for himself, a well-earned reward in honor of his promotion. Though in truth by the time Trysta whispered breathily into his ear that they were going to have a baby – "they" meaning she and Darren, not she and the plumber – their fling had grown into a thing, since by then they'd been sleeping together for weeks. Not that there'd been any actual sleeping, just whatever episodes of quick, hot sex they could sneak in on the loveseat sofa-bed in the new office that had been one of the perks of his promotion.

But at the time it had been nowhere on Darren's radar that their loveseat sex could result in the conception of a baby. The acts performed between himself and Trysta on that sofa-bed – or sometimes his desktop – were the stuff of every guy's porno dream come true, and surely not where babies or mothers of babies came from.

And yet there was Trysta, pressing her voluptuous breasts against him, whispering her news into his ear, her lovely blue eyes brimming with tears. But they were tears of joy and not of shame or remorse or fear of losing her plumber husband. On the contrary, she'd tearfully confided to Darren in an intimate moment immediately prior to their first coupling that her husband Silvio, coarse, brutish, working-class Neanderthal that he was, had lost interest in her long ago and that she hadn't felt a man's touch on her body in *years*. And how she was yearning, churning, *burning* for someone to…to…to…*make her feel like a real woman again.*

And so the breathily-delivered line that had compelled Darren to sweep this irresistibly horny woman off her feet and onto his office loveseat was the same line that kept it from occurring to him that Trysta's baby could possibly have been the product of the sperm of the brutish plumber Silvio Jablonski.

And yet Trysta's ex-husband Silvio didn't turn out to be such a brute that Darren's ex-wife Sally didn't fall in love with him, which Sally somehow did after she'd somehow met him. And which, truth be told, still kind of stuck in Darren's craw, especially after Silvio inherited his uncle's plumbing business and overnight morphed from a poor plumber into a rich plumber while Darren morphed from Vice-President of Strategic Acquisitions at Highland and Erskerberg into former Vice-President of Strategic Acquisitions at Highland and Erskerberg, laid-off, broke, and struggling to support a new wife, new house, new career move, new child-support payments for his own son, and a new baby on the way.

But at that moment, the moment when Trysta happily revealed that she and Darren were soon to be joined by the bonds of parenthood, it hadn't seemed so bad: Trysta's sparkling eyes, flushed cheeks, inviting lips, and now pregnant but still oh-so-willing body promised an eternal honeymoon drenched in domestic bliss and sex.

Of course there'd been the ordeal of his divorce from Sally. (Though he had figured there'd be some animosity on Sally's part, she'd taken the divorce a whole lot worse than he'd imagined she would, and apparently the lout Silvio hadn't taken the departure of his wife and children too well, either). But after Darren had gotten past all the unpleasantness with Sally and his pangs of regret at moving out on his six-year-old son Joshua, it had been great being with Trysta. Or at least it was until he was let go from Highland and Erskerberg after buying this big honking house out in in New Conshohocken for Trysta and her three wild kids, soon to be four.

And where had things gone from there? Darren decided to start his own real estate management business and, thanks to a couple of crap decisions he'd made while in the grip of financial desperation – and no thanks to the doings of his shit-for-brains step-brother Geoffry – he wound up where he now was, stuck by the balls in the dirty web of a crooked South Philly salvage yard operator named Angelo Barbieri. And yet, ironically, it was through Angelo Barbieri's patronage that

Darren's real estate management business began to take off. And it was also through Barbieri's influence with Jeremy Andrews, the CEO of Global Acquisitions at Highland and Erskerberg, that Darren was offered a contractor's job back at his old company. Darren could only guess how far across this city Barbieri's web stretched. And though the deals that Barbieri cut in Darren's behalf may have rescued him from economic disaster, they bound him ever more tightly to that web.

And how ironic was it that while Darren ended up stuck, Sally was free as a bird? And probably happy as one, too, with her rich plumber boyfriend Silvio Jablonski hanging around, likely spending all kinds of money on Sally and Josh while he, Darren, was being wrung dry from child support payments. And now, apparently, Sally had even adopted some little kid from Mexico, or Guatemala, or somewhere. Darren didn't know what *that* was all about, but if Sally wanted more kids, she was welcome to take over raising Trysta's Little Screamers.

As for Trysta, prodigious as was her talent for sex, she turned out to be less skilled when it came to parenting. And she'd definitely been a lot less fond of pregnancy than she was of the act that caused it.

Anyway, here Trysta was, still married to Darren and still making a play for her ex-husband Silvio even while the guy was about to slaughter her in a custody battle. Well, if Silvio wanted Trysta back along with his kids that would be fine with Darren. Trysta, her kids, this fucking over-priced albatross of a house in this fucking over-priced, cleared-away-scrub-field of a suburban Philadelphia housing development in New Conshohocken, this whole crazy, mixed-up mess that his life had become, he'd be glad to get away from it all.

But old Silvio wasn't having it. Oh, he wanted the kids back. Well, maybe not little Silvia Miri, not yet, anyway. But it sure wasn't looking like he wanted his ex-wife back. Hell, Silvio'd have to be crazy to trade Sally for Trysta. *I was crazy to trade Sally for Trysta,* Darren thought glumly.

He pictured Sally, with her dark, chin-length hair that she liked to pull back in a clip, her round dark brown eyes that could sparkle when she was happy or flash in anger, her small body that he could wrap his arms around, then he'd pull her close and cup her firm little backside in his hands. Sally. His first love. That is to say, his first love after his college girlfriend whom he'd been dating and sleeping with and talking marriage with for three years before he met Sally at an off-campus house party he'd gone to with his girlfriend. Darren smiled wistfully as he remembered Sally back then: a cute little twenty-year-old Catholic girl who was working, going to community college, and saving herself for marriage. And so one year later, barely out of college and his mouth watering for virginal Sally, he'd married her, and before they knew it Josh came along, unplanned, and then six years later Trysta came along, also unplanned, and now here they were.

Yes, Darren had been crazy to give up Sally for Trysta.

But then that's what Trysta did to men. Made them crazy. She was sure as fuck making Darren crazy these days. One day saying the baby was Silvio's, next day saying the baby was his, playing both ends against the middle, hedging her bets with both men so as to keep a roof over her head, and in the meantime plying Darren with so much sex – all right the sex was pretty great these days –and *that* was making him crazy, too.

"But *you're* making me craziest of all," he cooed to Silvia Miri, who smiled up at him and reached for his face. "Yes, that's right. You're the only one that I don't know what to do about yet. Everybody else is going back to Silvio and your mommy's gonna go, well, somewhere, because Daddy Darren is gonna tell her 'bye-bye.'" Darren held the baby close for a moment and whispered into her ear, "But your mommy doesn't know that yet, so don't you tell her." Silvia Miri giggled and Darren chuckled then continued, "And then Daddy Darren is gonna sell this house and get a nice little unit in Manayunk or Drexel Hill or somewhere, *alllll* to himself..." Darren sighed. "...and then there's somebody else Daddy's gotta figure out how to get away from ..." Darren looked away from the baby and muttered, "...without getting his legs broken." He looked around the room. "And if I'm gonna do that I sure as hell can't afford this life anymore." He looked back down at Silvia Miri. "But Daddy Darren is gonna find out whose baby you are and then we'll know what to do with you, yes we will."

Darren set Silvia Miri down in her Pack 'n Play then returned to his desk, opened the bottom drawer and reached into the back. He pulled out two home paternity testing kits that he'd picked up from Walmart.

"See?" He held up the kits for the baby to see, "Two different ones. So we'll know for sure." Then he picked up Silvia Miri and carried her over to the desk. "This will just take a minute. See, Daddy Darren is gonna swab inside your mouth, then inside his mouth, then we'll wrap up the swabs and put them back in the box, then Daddy Darren will fix you a nice bottle, then everything will be"

"Daddy Darren! We're *hungry!*"

"We're *hungry!* We're *starving!*"

Darren sighed. The Little Screamers were back in his office doorway.

"Okay, okay, Mommy will be home from the doctor's with Zach any minute then she'll fix supper."

"But we're starving *now!*" whined Trina.

"We're starving *right now!*" echoed her sister.

"Okay, look, go out to the kitchen and grab yourselves something, a yogurt, or an apple, or something."

"We don't *want* a yogurt or an apple!" whined Trina, "We want *you* to fix us some supper! Right now!"

"Yeah, we want our supper *right now!*" cried Sam, stamping her foot for emphasis.

"Yeah, well, I can't fix your supper now, I gotta, uh, do something in here first. So you go on to the kitchen and get yourselves something to eat, all right?"

"But we don't *want* to go to the kitchen by ourselves!" cried Trina, "We're *lonely!*"

"Yeah, we're *lonely!*" cried Sam, "And we're *scared!*"

Then the two burst into a loud wailing duet that became a trio when their hungry baby sister joined in.

"Okay, okay, Jesus!" Darren quickly dropped the two boxes back into his drawer then shepherded his wailing little flock out of his office and to the kitchen.

If I don't get the hell out of this insane asylum pretty soon Trysta's kid Zach isn't gonna be the only one who needs to see Dr. What's-Her-Face.

***

8

Dr. Laura Cavanni was forty-six years old, tall and slim with the lanky athletic build of a runner. She wore her long dark hair pulled back into a pony tail and her olive-toned skin was still smooth except for the laugh lines at the corners of her deep-set brown eyes. She had a wide, friendly smile and a big, deep-throated laugh that when she was in high school used to cause her friends to roll their eyes and say, "Geeze, Ali, you laugh like a guy!" ("Ali" had become Laura's nickname because of the jerk father of one of her teammates who went around saying that Laura looked like Ali MacGraw, some random actress from the 1970's. Laura didn't mind when her old high school friends once in a while teasingly called her "Ali," though it annoyed her when her ex-husband did).

Though Laura generally dressed business-casual for work – this day she was wearing a wide-striped black and white long-sleeved knit top with fitted black slacks and black ballet flats – one could imagine her in her element in gym clothes and running shoes. Laura Cavanni looked like someone who was captain of the field hockey team back in school, which she was, both in high school at the Shipley School in Bryn Mawr and in college at the University of Pennsylvania, where she also did her post-graduate work. She was also an accomplished horsewoman and she very much liked classical music.

Dr. Cavanni was pleased that the young patient sitting in front of her whom she'd recently been so concerned about seemed to be coming around, coping better, psychologically acclimating himself to what appeared to Dr. Cavanni to be an exceptionally chaotic family situation (and she'd seen many chaotic family situations, including her own at one time) no thanks to the child's mother, the striking young blonde woman sitting out in the waiting room whom Laura sized up as having a propensity for drama and for playing – unless she actually was – dumb.

"So, Zach, we'll aim for two weeks from today?" Laura asked her patient.

"Okay," said Zach. "We all done?"

"Yep," said Dr. Cavanni with a smile, "I think we pretty much covered all the bases. Unless you want to talk about anything else. Anything else? Questions? Anything?"

"Nope, I'm good." Zach stood and picked up his backpack.

"Good. I'll let your mom know about your next appointment."

"She's not gonna like it. She still hates you."

Laura laughed. "Oh, maybe she doesn't."

"Yep, she does."

As soon as Trysta heard the click of the office door handle she quickly put down the magazine she'd become absorbed in, crossed her arms, looked away from the door and pouted.

"So, Mrs. Miller," Dr. Cavanni said with a smile as she entered the waiting room, "Zach and I were thinking…" She caught sight of Trysta and her smile faded. *Yep, she does,* she thought with a sigh. "Zach," she said, "would it be okay with you if your mom and I talked for a minute in my office?"

Zach shrugged. "Sure." He flopped into one of the waiting room chairs and began rooting through his backpack.

"*Excuse me?*" huffed Trysta, finally looking at Dr. Cavanni, "Shouldn't you be asking *me*? I *am* his mother!"

"Oh, sorry, yes, of course. Do you have a minute, Mrs. Miller? To talk?"

"No, I do *not* have a minute." Trysta stood and slipped into her stylish black leather jacket then flung her purse over her shoulder. "I *happen* to have four children I have to get home and take care of. And by the way, some of us don't have time to sit around *talking* all day."

"*Mo-om,*" Zach groaned.

"No, it's all right, I understand," said Dr. Cavanni, thinking, *forget it, she's not budging.* "Zach, I'll see you in two weeks?"

"Sure," Zach replied, standing and slinging his backpack over his shoulder.

"Mrs. Miller," said Dr. Cavanni, handing Trysta an appointment card, "Zach and I were thinking we'd try going two weeks between appointments. That sound good?"

Trysta snatched the card from Dr. Cavanni's hand and dropped it into her purse without looking at it. "Fine. Whatever. Come, Zachary."

Laura followed them to the waiting room door. "On the other hand, I know that things have been a little turbulent at home, so if it turns out that"

"Things are *fine* at home thank you!" Trysta snapped.

"*Geeze*, Mom," Zach said between clenched teeth.

Dr. Cavanni crossed her arms, looked down, and sucked in her lips. Then she looked back up and smiled. "Okay, well, you know my number, right?"

"Right," said Zach.

"Mrs. Miller?"

Trysta spun around to face Dr. Cavanni. "I *told* you I do *not* have time for..."

She felt suddenly aware of Dr. Cavanni's eyes on her, studying her in a way that Trysta hadn't noticed the psychologist doing before, a way that made Trysta feel self-conscious, gave her the urge to pat her hair, check her face, ask this woman what she was looking at. Not that Trysta wasn't used to having the eyes of other women upon her, but she couldn't recognize in this woman's eyes any of the familiar looks, neither the hostility, confrontation, green-eyed jealousy or false cotton-candy friendliness of a rival, nor was it the too-familiar stare of disproval that Trysta had in truth been steeling herself against from the start with this woman. But there was no unfriendliness, or for that matter any friendliness, particularly, in those eyes, and certainly not a hint of the fawning admiration for her looks that Trysta was accustomed to seeing in the eyes of both men and women.

She just looked...*interested*. And focused today, for some reason Trysta couldn't fathom, on Trysta. "Well," Trysta said petulantly, "what did you want to talk about, anyway?"

"She wants to talk about *me*, Mom, okay?" Zach answered.

"*Ohhhh* maybe *not*, Mister," Laura teased, making a fist and pretending to give Zach a punch in the arm but stopping a millimeter short of making contact.

Though Trysta was suddenly piqued with desire to know what, if anything, this woman's interest in her might be other than in relation to her son, she made a show of tossing her long hair back behind one ear and putting a possessive arm around her son, who looked back and gave Dr. Cavanni a quick half-smile before leaving with his mother.

Laura Cavanni closed the door of her waiting room and headed back to her office whistling one of her favorite Gilbert and Sullivan ditties, "Things Are Seldom What They Seem."

When they were down the hallway from Dr. Cavanni's office Zach said to his mother, "You should talk to her. She's cool."

"*Humph,*" Trysta replied, glancing back over her shoulder, feeling the slightest twinge of disappointment that Dr. Cavanni wasn't standing in the hall still studying her as she walked away.

That night after yet another round of the tiring, joyless sex she'd been throwing herself into in desperation to keep Darren on the hook, Trysta lay in bed and contemplated that the attention in Dr. Cavanni's eyes today had been the most attention she'd felt from anyone in a long time.

***

The following week at ten am on Wednesday morning Trysta was sitting in Dr. Cavanni's office in a comfortable arm chair while the four-month-old baby girl whom she'd wanted to name Miri, just Miri, but didn't and now wished she had, slept in her carrier at Trysta's feet.

"I don't have much time," Trysta said coolly, "she'll be up soon."

"That's fine," replied Dr. Cavanni, who sat across from her in an upholstered leather desk chair. "You can feed her, change her, bounce her, whatever she wants, while we talk."

There passed a moment of silence between the two women.

"Well?" said Trysta impatiently.

"Well," replied Dr. Cavanni. She gazed steadily at Trysta with that same look of inscrutable interest. "How's your day going?"

"Huh?" The simple question caught her so off guard – how long had it been since anybody had cared how her day was going? – that Trysta instinctively paused to weigh the question and her answer. But Dr. Cavanni didn't press her. "My day is going how it *always* goes," Trysta snipped after a moment, "I'm up half the night with a crying baby who still wants to eat all the time and won't sleep, then I have to get up and get three children off to school, then I have to take care of the house, and the baby, and a husband, and, and, *everything!*"

"You're a busy, busy young mom," Dr. Cavanni replied with a sympathetic smile.

"Yes, I am," Trysta sniffed, "not that anybody appreciates it."

"Ah yes, a lot of lack of appreciation going around."

"Huh, tell me about it."

"Or *you* could tell *me* a little more about it," Dr. Cavanni coaxed, "if you want." She continued to study Trysta while Trysta twirled a lock of hair around her finger, glancing away from Dr. Cavanni then back again, the same posturing, the same suspicious expression Laura had seen in shy horses and wounded children.

Laura leaned slightly forward, folded her hands and rested them on her knees. "Anyway," she said, "you know I'm not your mom, right? Or your dad, or your husband or your ex-husband, or anybody's lawyer or social worker. What I'm saying is I just want you to know that I have no angles to play. Just so you know."

Trysta pulled in a couple of deep breaths, now reminding Laura of a nervous and not particularly eager freshman about to be sent out onto the hockey field. Then Trysta started speaking slowly, picking up speed and intensity until it seemed as if she were rolling out of control down an emotional hill. "See," she began, "I spend my whole life trying to *please* people, and make people *happy,* even when they don't *care* about *me,* and *now* I have to keep all these *children* happy, and *Darren* happy just so he doesn't kick me out, and my *father* happy so I can go back home in case Darren *does* kick me out, and *Silvio* thinks he doesn't want me anymore because of this, this *awful witch* that he lied to me about dating, and now *Silvio,* he's trying to take my children away and Darren's not even doing anything about it, and I've had too many children and too many husbands and I, I, *I hate them all!*"

At that moment the baby, awakened by the sudden crescendo of her mother's voice, began wailing and Trysta, horrified, realized what she'd just said. "Oh my God, oh my God," she cried, picking up her baby, "Oh my God, I didn't mean that! Mommy loves you," she cooed, holding her baby close. She looked at Dr. Cavanni, her eyes wide and filling with tears, "I didn't mean that, I *love* my baby! I love *all* my children!"

"I know," Dr. Cavanni replied gently, "It's all right."

Trysta stopped in mid-sob. "It is?"

"Of course. You're stressed, you're tired, you've got four children to look after and at the moment your future is perhaps looking a bit, well, precarious. Look, Trysta, here you can say anything you want."

"I can?" Trysta wiped a sleeve across her eyes.

Dr. Cavanni nodded.

"Oh." Trysta sighed. "Well, anyway, now I'll have to change her and feed her."

"Go right ahead," Dr. Cavanni said with a smile, "you're allowed."

After the baby was changed and happily latched onto Trysta's breast Trysta said, "I've never told anybody this, but – are you sure I'm allowed to say anything?" Dr. Cavanni nodded again and Trysta continued, "...but I never liked nursing. I just do it because it's more convenient. And cheaper."

"That it is," Dr. Cavanni chuckled.

The two women sat in silence for a moment then Trysta sighed, *"Men."*

"Men?"

"All they ever think about is their you-know-whats."

Dr. Cavanni nodded and smiled slightly.

"And all they want us for is *our* you-know-whats."

"Well," said Dr. Cavanni, "they do seem to like that sort of thing."

"Yeah. They do. And who gets stuck with the babies?"

Dr. Cavanni contemplated whether she should bring up the subject and then decided to do so, but carefully. "Um, Trysta...? Might there be some method of birth control that works well for you?"

"Birth control? Huh, you *see* how well it works! I had to marry Silvio at eighteen, then along comes Darren, Mr. Big Shot Company Vice-President of...Whatever. He *seduced* me away from Silvio and got me pregnant and then got himself *fired,* and then *Silvio* inherits his uncle's business, so now *he's* going to be rich, and *we're* practically broke." Trysta paused a moment then continued. "And then I realized," she gave a great sigh followed by another dramatic pause during which her eyes re-filled with tears, "that my baby wasn't Darren's after all, but Silvio's."

Dr. Cavanni blinked. "So you think, um, Miri...?" She tilted her head to get a better look at the happily nursing baby, "You think Miri is Silvio's daughter?" She handed Trysta the box of Kleenex on her desk.

"Yes," Trysta replied as she wiped her eyes, "I do."

Oh, no, Trysta, my blue-eyed child, Dr. Cavanni responded in her head, *this brown-eyed babe sure isn't the offspring of yourself and six-foot-two, eyes of blue Silvio, which he knows if he ever took sophomore biology.* To Trysta she said, "But maybe you're not one hundred-percent sure at this point?"

"Well, of *course* I'm…" Dr. Cavanni now sat with one elbow resting on the arm of her chair and her cheek resting against her hand, her deep eyes fixed on Trysta. Trysta sighed again, a stray tear running down her cheek. "The only one I'm sure she belongs to is me."

***

It was while she was in labor that it occurred to Trysta that passing off the baby as Silvio's right away – as opposed to taking a wait-and-see approach – was her best bet.

The labor nurse, probably just trying to jolly Trysta, distract her a little while she waited for the epidural to take effect, had asked about the baby's name.

"So what are we gonna name this little girl, huh?" the nurse asked, feeling Trysta's stomach then checking the IV line taped to her hand. "Try some deep breathing, Hon. We got a name picked out for this little princess?"

"Uhn, Uhn, Miri," Trysta gasped over the contraction.

"Miri," cooed the nurse, "how pretty."

"Miri Miller," said Darren from where he was nervously pacing the floor near the bed. "Sounds good."

"Well then, we'll be sure that's the name on the birth certificate," the nurse teased.

The name on the birth certificate. The name on the birth certificate. The words floated through the fog of semi-consciousness that settled over Trysta's brain as the anesthetic took effect. *Darren's name would be on the birth certificate!* She forced herself to wake up and focus. What if she decided to go with her plan to leave Darren, take her children and go back to Silvio? She knew at that moment that she had to make the decision right away, within the next twenty-four hours, before she left the hospital, before the birth certificate was signed. Otherwise what kind of kink would be caused by this legal document naming Darren as the father of this baby if she decided to go back to Silvio?

But of *course* she'd go back to Silvio! She wished Silvio were here right now instead of Darren. Silvio was so much calmer. Darren couldn't sit still. He could never sit still. And he yelled too much, at her and at the children.

But she'd have to get the ball rolling right away. Naming Silvio as the baby's father before the certificate was signed was a better idea though, Trysta knew, a daring one, in truth a desperate one, like the kind of play her father and brothers called a "Hail Mary" when they were watching an Eagles game and a cornered quarterback would throw a long pass in hopes that someone would catch it.

On the other hand Trysta knew that if there was one thing she excelled at, it was pulling off Hail Marys.

"Feeling better, Sweetie?" asked the nice nurse.

"Yes," Trysta replied. She always felt better when she had a plan.

The following day when Darren arrived to bring her home from the hospital she lay in bed, pale and wan from childbirth but with just a touch of blush and waterproof mascara, her long blonde hair freshly washed and brushed and falling over one shoulder. Her baby swaddled in her arms, her eyes glistening with tears, she gently confessed to Darren that this child was Silvio's, it couldn't be Darren's, it had arrived weeks too soon to be Darren's, and look at her little face, she was the image of Silvio. Though this child had brought Darren and Trysta together in love (Trysta thought this line, which she'd thought up herself, was quite touching), Trysta could not lie, she *could* not, and she couldn't live with herself if she did. This child was Silvio's and, for the child's sake and for the sake of honesty and legality, Silvio's name as the father must be on her birth certificate. And she could not be named Miri, as Trysta had wanted, had wanted with all her heart; no, for the sake of truthfulness and, and *rightfulness*, this child *deserved* to be named *Silvia*, after her father. The tears spilled over Trysta's eyes and down her cheeks, and she imagined what a beautiful scene this would be in a movie, not to mention the insurance the hospital room location afforded that Darren wouldn't be able to fly too horribly off the handle.

But Darren, after a moment of drop-jawed and tongue-tied astonishment, took the news much better than she'd expected. To her surprise and, in truth, her annoyance, Darren had no problem at all with leaving his name off the birth certificate; in fact he insisted that they call Silvio right away to give him the good news and — who knew? Silvio being Silvio — maybe even get him over to the hospital to meet his new daughter, named after him, even — how would that big old kid-loving softie Silvio be able to resist *that?* — and put his name on the birth certificate.

Trysta, her voice trembling and teary, made the call to Silvio on Darren's phone, with Darren listening in on speaker in case he should be needed to assist with the operation.

But the phone call lasted less than two minutes and all Silvio had to say was, "Trysta, whatever you're doing, stop it."

"Great, just great," Darren had said as he shoved his cell phone back into his pocket. "So tell me, Trysta, just what the fuck *are* you doing?"

But Trysta, baby in her arms, just sobbed and sobbed.

***

Though up to this point in her career Laura Cavanni had heard manys the confusing, convoluted, and downright bizarre tale of the foibles of human interactions and behavior, this one was, as her Philadelphia blue-blooded father would say, a humdinger of a sticky-wicket. "So then what happened?" she asked Trysta.

"It was such a mess," Trysta sniffled. "I figured Silvio just needed some time. So I wrote 'Silvia Miri Jablonski' on the birth certificate and I signed it but Darren wouldn't sign it even though the lady in the hospital office told him he had to because we were married, but he told them this wasn't his baby so he wasn't going to sign it and I asked her if we could just leave that space blank and she said okay but then treated me like I was...*trash,* or something."

No kidding, thought Laura. "But Silvio has never come around?" she asked.

"No. And I found out why soon enough." Trysta detached Silvia Miri from her breast and began patting her back. "Because of Sally. Darren's awful ex. She seduced my husband."

"You mean…your *ex*-husband. After you were already divorced. Right?"

"Well…yes. But if not for her Silvio would take me back in a minute, I know he would. It's me he always loved. Sally went after him just to spite me."

"Hm," said Laura. "But back to the birth certificate…was it ever signed? By Darren?"

"No. The lady at the hospital said it could be signed later. Whenever I figured out who the father was. She was such a witch!"

"Umm-hmm," said Dr. Cavanni. "You know, it would be easy enough to figure out who the father actually is." To herself she added, *if it served your purposes to figure it out, which it obviously doesn't at this moment.* She continued, "Look, somebody's going to have to pay support for this child. Who's supporting her now?"

"Darren, of course. She's Darren's daughter." Trysta laid Silvia Miri on her knees and began playing with the baby's hands.

"Wait, she's *Darren's* daughter?"

"Well…Darren's or Silvio's."

Dr. Cavanni sighed.

"But I'll *never* let Silvio have her! I'll never let him have *any* of my children!" Trysta paused and then added, "Not unless he takes me, too."

"Okay," said Dr. Cavanni. "Well, our session is about over. You did well."

"I did?"

Dr. Cavanni nodded and smiled, and her smile, her words, those deep eyes still fixed on Trysta as if they were looking into her soul, gave Trysta a sudden strange fluttery sensation in her chest, like butterfly wings fluttering around her heart.

"But there's something I want you to think about before our next session," Dr. Cavanni continued, and for Trysta, hearing that she would see this woman again, the only person she could really, truly pour out her aching heart to, caused her a little thrill of happiness.

"What would you like me to think about, Doctor?" she asked, a slight girlish lilt in her voice.

Dr. Cavanni tilted her head thoughtfully. "Trysta, I'd like to know why you're fighting so hard for what you don't want."

Chapter Two

It was a little past eight pm. Sally had just tucked Joshua in for the night and was rocking David while feeding him his evening bottle when Silvio stopped by after a long day at work. There were many long days since Silvio had taken over his uncle's business, Quick and Reliable Plumbers. But of course that was actually a good thing, and even the long days didn't stop Silvio from stopping by Sally's condo often; anymore it was getting to be almost every night, so that Sally'd returned to her habit of leaving her front door unlocked in the evening, not from forgetfulness as before, but for Silvio.

This night Silvio entered carrying a bakery box tied with a festive pink ribbon.

"What the heck?" Sally laughed, her face lighting up with a smile.

"We gotta celebrate," said Silvio, setting the box on Sally's dinette table.

"What are we celebrating? My birthday? Because I'll tell you, right now I feel like I just turned eighty, or something. Little stinkerdoodle here got me up again last night."

"Yeah, well you look tired, all right. Here, gimme that stinkerdoodle." Silvio reached down to take David and the bottle from Sally's arms.

"I don't know, he might cry," Sally said as she nonetheless handed the child to Silvio then stood and stretched.

"Nah, he likes his Tio Silvio, don't you, Majeito?" he said, calling the baby by the Nicaraguan slang word for "little dude" that David's father

Ascensión Guzman used to call his son. And the baby did in fact break into a chubby-cheeked smile as he reached for Silvio.

With David on his lap Silvio settled into the rocking chair, a wide, comfy, upholstered Lullaby Glider he'd bought for Sally shortly after she became David's foster mother. He ran a hand over the ten-month-old's curly black hair. "How come you're waking Tia Sally up at night, huh?"

"Maybe he misses his real mommy," said Sally, eyeing the box on the dinette table.

"Yeah, well...hey, go ahead and open it," Silvio said, nodding towards the box, "it's for you."

"Okaaay...So wha'd I do to deserve this?" Sally looked pleased as she carefully untied the pink ribbon around the box.

"You know."

"No, I d...Oh, you!" Sally broke into a laugh at the big swirled "A+" written in red icing on a small round vanilla-frosted layer cake edged with yellow and blue roses.

"I got it at Hegley's, you know that bakery your mom is always going on about. I told them it was special so could they wrap it up nice and they tied that ribbon on it for me."

Sally felt her eyes filling. "Oh, you," she said softly, hurrying back to the rocking chair and bending to caress Silvio's face and kiss his cheek. "You are just too much!"

Silvio stood and hugged Sally with one arm while he held David in the other. "Well, you finish your first course at Temple U. with an 'A-plus,' somebody's gotta do something about it."

"It was only an "A," Sally chuckled.

"All the extra work you had to do, I mean working full time and taking care of these kids on your own, and all, you deserve an 'A-plus.' You know you're gonna be the smartest lawyer in Philadelphia, right?"

Sally laughed. "Or at least the oldest. *If* I survive college. And then law school after that."

"You will," said Silvio. "With flying colors."

"Aw," Sally said, snuggling as close to Silvio as she could with the baby between them. "And by the way, I haven't been on my own. I couldn't have done it without you. Thank you, Silvio. For the cake. And everything."

"It's me who should be thanking you," said Silvio. "I don't know what I'd do without you, Sally."

"Or me without you. Crazy as it all is."

Baby David threw his empty bottle to the floor and reached for Sally who took him from Silvio and showed him the cake on the table. "Look at the pretty cake Tio Silvio got for Tia Sally for getting an 'A' in her class."

"He wants a piece of that," Silvio chuckled.

"Well," Sally cooed to David, kissing his cheek, "he'll just have to wait until tomorrow, won't he?" David laughed with delight at the animation in Sally's face and voice as she continued, "Yes, tomorrow you'll get a *greaaaat* big piece, and your big *hermano* Joshie will get a *greaaat* big piece…"

Silvio came up behind Sally and put his hands on her waist and kissed her neck. "How about Tio Silvio?"

Sally turned to Silvio and sighed. "Well, let me see if I can get little Majeito here down for the count. You want me to make some coffee? To go with the cake?"

"Nah, maybe just some milk."

"You want to cut yourself a piece while I rock him?"

"Nope. I'll wait."

Silvio stretched out on Sally's couch while she rocked David.

"You gonna fall asleep on me?" she asked.

"I'm tired enough to."

"Shoot, me too."

"I'd rather fall asleep with you. Every night, not just the nights when Darren has Josh."

"Aw, Silvio," Sally said, "you know how it is, I mean, I know everybody lives together, and all, but I just don't feel right about you spending the night when Josh is here, even though he loves you and you're a better dad to him these days than Darren is. Still, I mean, what would my mom say, she's so religious and old-fashioned, and your mom is, too, and with everything going on, you being in the middle of your custody battle, and what if"

"Marry me, Sally," Silvio cut her off.

"Huh?" Sally stopped in mid-rock.

"Marry me. Right now."

"What? Right *now*?"

Silvio sprung from the couch and grabbed the cake from the table then he got down on one knee facing Sally, holding the cake out before her. "Marry me. Never mind about the kids and our moms and our exes, and our troubles. I'll buy us a big house in Cornwells Heights, or the Northeast, or wherever you want, big enough for you and me and all the kids. I got the money now, and our moms'll help us out like they always do, and we'll make it work, Sally, I promise we will. I love you so much. Marry me, Sally. Will you marry me?"

Sally's eyes glistened with tears. Holding onto the baby with one hand she reached for the cake with the other and scooped up a fingerful of icing, hesitated, then rubbed it onto Silvio's cheek. Then she bent towards him and licked it off. "Yes, I'll marry you."

Silvio set the cake down onto the floor and rubbed a sleeve across his eyes. Still kneeling, he likewise dipped his finger into the icing, rubbed it across Sally's cheek and licked if off. Then he wrapped his strong arms around her waist and buried his face in her knees.

"How about," said Sally, "I get our little friend here down then you and me can take the cake into the bedroom and have some more icing. You know, like we did that one time? Would you like that?"

Silvio nodded, his face still buried in Sally's knees.

***

"Darren, *why* don't you help me with these children?" Trysta stood in the doorway of Darren's office looking cross, baby in her arms and flanked by Sam and Trina.

"Yeah, Darren, why don't you help Mommy get us to bed?" said Sam, mimicking her mother's intonation.

"Geeze, what are you a bunch of babies?" Zach came up behind his mother and sisters. "Why can't you get yourselves to bed?"

"Look you guys, I'm busy, I'm trying to run a business, I got something important to"

"Mommy!" Trina cried, "Zach called us a baby! He always calls us a baby!"

"Mommy, he always calls us a baby!" cried Sam.

"Yeah, 'cause you are," snapped Zach.

"Darren, I *said*, could you *please*"

"Oh, fine, give me the baby," Darren cut off his wife, taking the baby from her arms. "Sam, Trina, go on and brush your teeth!"

"We want a snack!"

"We want a snack!"

"No more snacks! And no more crying! Zach, get your sisters into the bathroom and make sure they brush their teeth."

"What?" cried Zach, indignity personified, "*I* have to do it?"

"You're what, twelve now?"

"Yeah?"

"So you're old enough to start being in charge, right?"

Zach looked momentarily bewildered then pleased by his newly acquired status. "Fine," he nonetheless huffed, "come on, you guys, go get ready for bed!"

"Tell Zach he's not allowed to push us!"

"And he has to read us a story!"

"Fine, come on," Zach said, herding his sisters down the hallway and up the stairs, "and just one freakin' book, okay?"

"No, two!" The girls continued wheedling as the group disappeared at the top of the stairs.

"First brush your freakin' teeth!" Zach's voice traveled down from upstairs.

"Hey, Zach, watch that language around your sisters, you hear?" Darren called up.

"Fine!" Zach called down.

"All right," Darren said to Trysta, "you want me to feed this baby now or are you going to? Because I got things to do yet tonight, you know?"

Trysta stood with her arms crossed, though looking kind of good, Darren thought, in the dark green turtle neck and snug jeans she was wearing, her blonde hair cascading over one shoulder. "She needs to learn how to take a bottle at night," Trysta answered, then she walked away, turning back to add, "And *you* need to watch *your* language around the children. Zach certainly isn't learning that language from *me*."

"*The fuck?*" Darren mumbled. What the hell was eating Trysta? The past few days she'd been in a mood, kind of bitchy and demanding and keeping to her own side of the bed and saddling him with the kids, the baby – *her* kids, *her* baby – when he had work to do and she had…*what* to do that she couldn't even nurse her baby? What the hell was eating her all of a sudden, anyway?

Fine, he'd feed the baby. Huh, if Trysta was in a bitchy mood now, just wait until Silvio got her kids – when was the hearing, a couple of weeks from now? And speaking of Silvio…"Come on, we'll get you your bottle," he said to the baby, "and then we're gonna call your daddy."

***

Silvio and Sally lay in bed, sticky and wrapped in each other's arms while what was left of the cake and its demolished icing sat on Sally's dresser.

"Why don't we do this more often?" Silvio asked, licking a stray bit of blue frosting from Sally's cheek.

Sally laughed softly. "Well, besides the fact that it's a mess, I can think of *five* little reasons why we don't do this more often. And once you have your kids back – hopefully …"

"Oh, I'll get 'em back, all right."

"I know you will. And then when all seven of us are living in our nice, big house out in Cornwells Heights, or wherever, fat chance of us having dessert in bed like this. Or much time at all together, crazy as it's gonna be, the kids, your work, my school…"

"I'll always have time for you, Sally. No matter how many kids we end up with or how crazy it gets. And hey, I'll help you change these sticky sheets."

"Aw, you don't have to. Since you've still got to get home tonight," Sally pressed a finger on a spot of icing on Silvio's chest, "*and* take a shower!"

Silvio heaved a sigh. "We're engaged now, right?"

"We are. I can't believe it."

"So doesn't that make things different? About me spending the night, I mean."

Sally sighed. "Aw, Silvio, it's not you spending the night, it's Josh finding you in my bed. *Before* we're married."

"Well then we better hurry up and get married."

"We better. Before we got those five kids between us."

"Those five kids will bring us together. It's like I told you, Sally, I'll never let anything come between us."

At that moment Silvio's cell phone rang. "Aw, I better get up and see who that is," he said, "could be an emergency and I'm on call tonight. Eh, never mind, it stopped ringing."

"How's your 24-hour plumbing service working out?"

"Not too bad. Makes us a lot of money. If only I had a couple more good plumbers on board. To spread the shifts."

"Well, hopefully you'll have Ascensión on board pretty soon. As soon as his work certification comes through he and Lupe can come back here from Nicaragua, then they can pick up their little David from me, and you'll have your Spanish-speaking plumber for all your Hispanic customers."

"I don't know. You know how things have been going in Nicaragua lately. The rioting in the capital, and all."

"I know," said Sally, "and it worries me. I try not to think about it."

"Yeah, better not to. But speaking of which, have you heard from Ascensión and Lupe lately?"

"Not lately," said Sally. "The email and cell service down there still go out sometimes for days. But you remember how I told you that I was able to FaceTime them about a week and a half ago and the picture was all blocky and the sound wasn't too good. And then with Ascensiòn's English being what it is…"

"But you got that things are a little better in León now."

"Yeah, I did get that," said Sally. "At least I think that's what Ascensión was telling me. And I got that he and Lupe are still working at those jobs they got in the jungle outside León with that American engineering company trying to figure out how to, I don't know, heat water systems from the volcanoes, or something."

"Well, then, if the Americans are still there then it must not be all that bad."

"I know, but...I couldn't tell for sure because the video and sound were so sketchy, but I thought maybe Lupe was crying."

"Aw, gee," sighed Silvio. "Well, and at least she knows that her baby is safe and happy and getting enough to eat, and all."

"And that he's with people who love him," said Sally.

"That's for sure," said Silvio.

"Silvio," Sally said, holding him closer, "I always try to be optimistic and act like I believe that the Guzman's are coming back. But sometimes what I really think is that Lupe and Ascensión aren't gonna make it back up here any time soon. I mean, with what's going on in Nicaragua and what's going on here in this country, I mean how it's going for immigrants these days...I just don't know."

Silvio kissed Sally's forehead. "I don't know what's gonna happen either. But we're all doing our best. And we all have each other. And most important, I have you. And nothing's ever gonna change...aw, rats, there goes my phone again." Silvio sighed. "Let me go get it."

Silvio climbed out of bed and picked up his phone from where he'd left it next to his wallet and keys on Sally's dresser. "Huh," he said, looking at the name of the missed call on his screen, "it's Darren."

"*Tsk*, what's he want?"

"Well, I don't know. He didn't leave a message, or anything." Silvio considered for a moment. "I better call him back. In case it's one of my kids, or something."

Silvio slipped into his jeans then sat on the edge of Sally's bed and called Darren.

"What's going on?" Silvio asked after Darren answered. Silvio listened for a minute then his face screwed into a look of disbelief. "*What?* No, that's...that's not...no, wait, that's *crazy*, that's...I don't...*No!*" Silvio listened in silence then he asked, "Did you tell Trysta yet...? Oh, well, that's great, she's gonna...So you're not gonna tell her...?" He listened for a few more moments then finally said in a flat tone, "You'll send me the test results. Yeah. Yeah, I understand. Yeah." His thumb hit his phone then he sat in silence on the edge of the bed.

"Silvio, Honey, what is it?" Sally moved next to him and caressed his shoulders.

Silvio turned to her, a look of shock on his face. "Darren took a paternity test. Silvia isn't his."

Sally gasped. After a few moments of silence she said, "You don't think she's…"

Silvio took Sally's hand. "Mine."

***

Trysta sat at her vanity table brushing her hair and studying herself in the mirror. She'd shut the bedroom door against the noise of her children, who were bickering themselves to bed. Darren was right. Zachary was old enough to start helping her more. And the girls at seven and nine years old should be able to get themselves to bed. *She* was certainly expected by her ex-marine father to toe the line by the time she was their age. Let everyone learn to start taking care of themselves instead of expecting her to be their slave. "I'm thirty years old," she said softly to herself in the mirror. "Darren's going to leave me. Silvio's going to take my children." Her eyes filled with tears. "I'll have to take Miri and go back and live with my parents and go back to work." She suddenly felt the desire to be holding her baby girl close right now. Her Miri. The only one who loved her. Still, Trysta didn't particularly feel like feeding her and putting her to bed at this moment. Let Darren do it. Let him get used to taking care of Miri so that he'd get attached to her and forget what Trysta had said before about her being Silvio's daughter and think of her as his own. Because Miri *had* to be Darren's daughter. Who else would support her if not Darren? How could she support her baby on an office receptionist's pay?

Maybe she'd do better as a waitress. A waitress in a fancy downtown Philadelphia restaurant, a really classy place in Center City or Society Hill or Headhouse Square. Someplace where powerful corporate men went for business lunches and dinners and left spectacular tips to friendly, sexy waitresses.

Trysta stood and looked herself over, head to toe. She flipped back her hair and smiled her most appealing smile. "Hi there," she said to some imaginary well-dressed middle-aged man, "can I get you a drink? What would you like, Sir?" Then her smile faded and she dropped back down into her chair. She dropped her head into her hands for a moment, her long hair falling forward over her face. Then she looked back up into the mirror and asked her reflection, "Why do I fight so hard for what I don't want?"

Chapter Three

"Free at last, free at last, da dee da dee da dee da, I'm free at last!" Darren tapped out the rhythm on the steering wheel even though he couldn't remember all the words to the song; well, it had been twenty years ago back in middle school music class that he'd learned that song and who ever paid attention in middle school music class? Still, he felt like singing. It was just a matter of time now. He'd wait to sell the house until Silvio got the kids, though maybe he should put the house on the market now since the final custody hearing was coming up already and maybe it would take some time to sell that fucking monster of a suburban McMansion.

That thought brought him down and reminded him where he was headed: To South Philly for a butt-fucking by that crass three-quarters Mafioso who owned a shady salvage yard, a bunch of good Philadelphia properties, Darren's soul, and who knew what else.

Darren pulled off Oregon Avenue into the lot of Angelo Barbieri's warehouse.

He was buzzed into the warehouse and greeted by Dina, Barbieri's receptionist who smiled at Darren then buzzed for the elevator from her desk. "Go ahead on up, Hon."

Darren took the elevator to the second floor then knocked on the fine mahogany door of Barbieri's office.

"Come *ii-in*," sang a voice from the other side.

Aw, screw me, Darren thought. He pulled in a deep breath then opened the door to see his step-brother Geoffry behind Angelo

Barbieri's desk, lounging back in Barbieri's chair, his stocking feet on the polished desk as if he owned it.

"What are you, *nuts?*" Darren gasped. "Where's Barbieri? He sees you like that he'll grab your tongue and wrap it around your balls!"

Geoffry laughed and removed his feet from the desk. "He's down the hall in the can."

"What do you mean down the hall? His bathroom's right there," Darren pointed to a door next to a far corner of the office, "he's got a shower in it and everything."

Geoffry shrugged. "He likes to take a shit in the other bathroom down the hall. Go figure."

"Yeah, well, that's great, but you better get your ass the hell out of his chair."

Geoffry stood, pushed the chair back closer to the desk and rubbed his sleeve on the desk where his feet had been. "There," he said as he put on his shoes, "you happy now, Mom?"

"I'm not your fuckin' mom," Darren mumbled.

"What?" said Geoffry.

"What the hell did you do to your hair?" said Darren. "You look like Donald Trump Junior."

"Hey that's just what *I* said!" Angelo Barbieri was standing in his doorway tucking his pale blue checked Brooks Brothers shirt into his expensive tan size forty-two husky Regent-Fit trousers. "His hair all slicked back like that, doesn't he look like Donald Junior now? Or wait, not Donald Junior, but the other kid, the blonde guy, what's-his-name, the one looks like there's nobody home, you know who I mean?"

"Yeah, I don't know," said Darren. "Jason, or something,"

"That's who you look, like," Angelo Barbieri said, walking over to the men and slinging an arm around grinning Geoffry's shoulders, "Jason Trump." Barbieri lightly poked Geoffry's stomach where it bulged over his belt. "Gettin' a little *grassone*, there, huh, Jason? You don't lay off the *pasta fazzoule* you'll have a lard ass on you like your daddy Donald." Angelo broke into a loud guffaw shared by Geoffry. Angelo pointed to Geoffry. "Ya see, Bobby Darren?" he said, calling Darren by the nickname he'd pinned on him, "Jason Trump here's got a great sense of humor, that's why everybody loves the guy." Barbieri turned back to Geoffry. "Whataya say, J.T.? Can we get your brother here to loosen up a little? He's standing there looking like he's got a Popsicle up his can."

"He needs to warm it up in his wife's hot cooch," replied Geoffry.

"This guy," laughed Angelo, again poking Geoffry's stomach, "is he a *paisan' oobatz*, or what?"

Darren stood with a tight forced smile stretched across his face while Angelo and Geoffry yucked it up.

Barbieri released Geoffry's shoulder then said, "Aw, J.T. what are we gonna do with Bobby Darren, here? He just doesn't like to make the *battut'*. You gotta work on this guy. Hey you got that cash ready for him? And the checks?"

"Yeah, it's in my desk, there," said Geoffry. "You want me to go get it?"

Angelo looked blankly at Geoffry for a moment then he ran a hand over his bald head and said, "Yeah, Jason Trump, go get it." While Geoffry was pulling the envelopes of money from the desk drawer with his back to the room Angelo leaned close to Darren and said softly, "You musta got all the brains in the family." Then to Geoffry he called, "Hey never mind, leave it there. You and D can count it at your desk." To Darren he said, "Look at that nice desk I got for your brother, I let him put it by the window, gives him a great view of the Navy Yard." To Geoffry he called, "You like that desk, J.T.?"

"Oh, yeah," Geoffry answered.

"You want me to get you your own desk, Bobby D.?"

"No thanks," Darren replied tersely.

"Aw, you know I'm just dickin' you. You go over and count the money with your bro, there."

Without moving Darren asked, "Uh, Angelo...what's this money about?"

"What's it about? Whataya mean what's it about? It's what it's always about. I got some money, you need some money, right?" Angelo chuckled. "Okay." He motioned Darren to the other side of the room and spoke softly enough to be out of Geoffry's earshot. "There should be about a hundred and ten over there, some checks, some cash, some money orders, like always, right? You go and buy me some piece of shit somewhere, out in North Philly, West Philly, Germantown, I don't care, just not Wedgefield, okay? You won't make crap on a flip in Wedgefield. But go buy me something somewhere else, then sell it and bring me back the money. Go ahead and take your commission today, I'll give you ten percent, you like that, D.? Take it out in advance, I don't care, I know you're good."

Forget it, Barbieri, I'm through laundering your dirty money for you, go find some other stooge to do your shit work, I'm outta here, was what Darren said to Angelo Barbieri in his mind. "Yeah, okay," he mumbled then he walked across the room and sat down at the desk next to Geoffry, who'd shaken the money from several envelopes out onto his desk.

As if reading Darren's mind Angelo called, "Unless you're too busy over there at Highland and Erskerberg. They giving you too much work over there these days? Should I call over there to Jeremy Andrews and tell him to cut you back a little?" Angelo chuckled. "Whataya say, should I call my buddy Jeremy?"

"That's okay, I'm good," Darren said, trying not to give away in his voice the knot in his stomach.

"Great. Start counting there, Bobby D. You count it, too, J.T."

Darren and Geoffry each pulled up the calculators on their phones and began counting the money before them in silence while Darren's mind whirled. *A couple of back-room petty low-lifes, a couple of street whores in bondage to this pimp, Barbieri's prisoners, Barbieri's stooges, Barbieri's fall guys, the idiots who'll wind up in prison for this stupid shit while Barbieri skips off and pockets the change, I gotta get outta here, I gotta, somehow, I gotta,*

"Hey, look at you two," Angelo called over from his desk where he sat checking some receipts, "*I due fratelli,* the two brothers. Hey, Bobby Darren, whyncha take Jason Trump on board your business? He could do you some good."

Yeah, right, Darren thought, *like that amateur fuck-up could do me any...* the idea hit him like a small jolt of electricity to the brain. *Yeah,* he thought looking into the vacuous eyes of his snickering step-brother. Darren smiled at Geoffry. *Yeah, okay, maybe I will, Brother.*

Chapter Four

Sally and Silvio sat close next to each other in the law office of Charleston Tilley. Silvio held Sally's hand and played absently with her fingers. Charleston Tilley leaned forward in his chair, his elbows propped on his desk, his chin resting on his folded hands. He listened while Silvio and Sally related the latest chapter in the continuing saga of their ever-complicated lives. Though he'd been practicing family and immigration law for a good thirty-five years and thought he'd seen every possible variation, for better or worse, on the theme of human behavior, these two white kids always had something new to add to his resume of experience.

He'd never forget the first day they showed up at his office, the thirty-year-old plumber and his twenty-seven-year-old girlfriend, nervous, good-hearted working-class youngsters with a convoluted story about a couple of undocumented Nicaraguan immigrants with an American-born baby whose lives had become intertwined with their own and on whose behalf they were seeking his help.

And he had taken on their case pro bono, as he did from time with poorer clients whose plights kept him from ever forgetting the young black man he'd once been, young and powerless and at the mercy of a justice system that was far from blind to color, wealth and influence. Still, Charleston had been unprepared for the ball of complications that led them all down a legal rabbit hole from which they'd emerged more fortunate than they might have, thanks to a sensible immigration judge and Silvio and Sally's generosity. Ascensión and Lupe Guzman were voluntarily deported back to Nicaragua with no ensuing U.S. Immigration penalties while they waited for the permanent labor certification that Silvio, as a business owner, had filed under Charleston's direction in hopes of hiring Ascensión on to his plumbing company. Then to the astonishment of everyone, himself not least, Sally stepped up to become the temporary guardian of the Guzman's now ten-month-old baby, David.

But Charleston's involvement with Sally and Silvio had hardly ended with the disposition of the case of the Nicaraguan immigrants. They were themselves in need of a legal advocate for their own problems, but Good Lord, would it ever be a simple case with these two?

Charleston unfolded his hands and placed them on his desk. "So what you're telling me, Mr. Jablonski," he said, "is that, based on Darren Miller's negative paternity test, the results of which he has forwarded to you, you believe that you are the father of your ex-wife's baby?"

"Well, yeah."

Charleston paused thoughtfully for a moment then continued. "What I don't understand is why Darren not being the father necessarily makes *you* the father."

"See, that's what *I* said," Sally interjected.

"Who else *could* the father be?" said Silvio, sounding slightly irritated. "I mean, she worked all day, came home at night, when the heck would she have had *time* for, you know, anybody else?"

"Same way she had time for Darren," Sally replied, also sounding slightly irritated.

"I mean somebody else *besides* Darren," said Silvio.

"If Trysta could cheat on you she could cheat on Darren," said Sally, then she turned to Charleston. "Right, Mr. Tilley?"

"It does seem within the realm of possibility. But the fact that your ex-wife's husband has informed you that he's not the father of her child means nothing to you at this point. And paternity test notwithstanding, in the state of Pennsylvania Darren is still the putative father – the legal father, that is – because the child was born within his marriage to Trysta."

"*Really?*" Silvio and Sally asked together.

35

"Yes. Darren cannot simply repudiate his paternity of this child just because of a store-bought paternity test."

"Huh," said Sally. "Boy, is he gonna be surprised."

"In truth, Mr. Jablonski, at this moment the ball's in your court."

"Oh," Silvio replied blankly.

"Look," Charleston continued, "it doesn't matter whether Darren is or isn't the father of the child. The only way that he could be potentially legally absolved of his paternal responsibilities is if another man – such as yourself – were to successfully challenge Darren's paternity by not only proving his own paternity but convincing the judge that he would be by far the more desirable father to the child. So if you wish to ignore this," Charleston gestured towards the copy of the paternity test that Darren had emailed to Silvio, "you can."

"See?" said Sally, "You can just ignore it."

"But...I mean...what if I *am* the father?"

"Well..." Charleston pulled in a deep breath. "Can I ask you something, Mr. Jablonski?"

Silvio shrugged. "Sure. Anything."

"What is *your* intention, that is, the outcome you wish for yourself regarding this child – what is her name?"

"Silvia," replied Silvio, reddening.

Charleston drew back in disbelief. "Did you just say...*Silvia?* Your ex-wife named her husband's baby *Silvia?* After...*you?*"

"I know, do you believe it?" said Sally, the words tumbling out as if they'd been under pressure for too long. "And then Trysta calls Silvio the day after the baby's born to tell him that she made a mistake, the baby's really *his*, I mean do you *believe* that?"

Charleston shook his head in confusion.

"Oh, well, of course," Sally continued, "it's because Silvio's coming into a lot of money now, I mean with him inheriting his Uncle Bud's business he's probably making more money now than Darren, who she tore apart *her* family and *mine* for to get her greedy little paws on *Darren's* money, but now"

"Sally," Silvio interrupted.

"But now," Sally rolled on, ignoring Silvio's interruption, "now she's not happy with Darren anymore, she's not happy with her fancy house in her fancy neighborhood and all her fancy…*stuff*, *now* she's back in *my* life, making a play to get Silvio back, never mind about other people's lives, other peoples…*hearts*…why won't she just, just… *leave me alone?*"

"Aw, Sally, Honey, come on," Silvio said gently, caressing her hand.

"Here, Mrs. Miller," said Charleston, also gently, handing Sally a small box of Kleenex he'd taken from his desk drawer.

"Oh, geeze, am I crying?" Sally touched the wet streak running down her cheek. "Sorry," she sniffed, reaching for a Kleenex.

Charleston then proffered the Kleenex box to Silvio. "Help yourself, Mr. Jablonski."

Silvio hesitated but Sally reached for another Kleenex and wiped Silvio's brimming eyes. "It's okay, Honey," she said.

"Indeed it is," added Charleston with a smile. "You'll notice the box is nearly empty. I do run up quite a Kleenex bill."

"Well then, I'll take another one," sniffed Silvio, who took two and handed one to Sally.

"Anyway," said Sally, daubing her eyes again, "you see what Trysta does to people."

"Maybe it would be best at this point for you to take some time to answer for yourself a few questions, including the one I started to ask you earlier: Do you want to get involved, Mr. Jablonski? Do you want to know if the child is yours? If so, what outcome would you like to see in this rather, uh, potentially…*byzantine* situation? What outcome if the child were yours? What outcome if the child weren't? Figure it out…between yourselves, I'd suggest. Then come back and we'll decide upon a plan of action. Does that sound good?"

Silvio looked down at his hands, still wrapped around Sally's. "Yeah. I guess."

Sally sighed.

"Look Mr. Jablonski and Mrs. Miller, these custody battles can be"

"From hell," Sally cut in.

"Exactly," said Charleston. "But try to bear with it. I know you both already have much on your plates even without heaping on this new complication. But if I may give you some personal advice?"

"Sure," said Sally.

"Yeah, I think we could use some advice," added Silvio.

"All right, then. Try not to let this situation come between you. Whatever your exes say or do, do *not* let it divide you. Do not let their problems become yours. And be patient. What's going on at this moment is really only temporary, even though it might be some time before the situation is normalized."

"Like, how much time?" said Silvio.

"Come back and tell me what you want to happen. Then we'll pick a wishful target time."

In the elevator down from Charleston's office Silvio took Sally's hand.

"So what do you want to do?" she asked him.

"Aw geeze, I can't even think straight," he said. After a few moments of silence he asked her, "What do you want me to do?"

"I don't know either."

"Only...what if little Silvia *is* mine?"

"And what if she isn't?"

They walked in silence for a few moments then Silvio stopped and said, "I gotta find out."

"If you do then you do."

He looked into Sally's eyes. "And if she's mine..."

"Then we'll go get another crib for our new house."

"Aw, Sally..."

When the elevator reached the first floor and the doors slid open the crowd of people waiting to enter were surprised by the sight of a big muscular man and a small slender woman wrapped in a tight embrace.

Chapter Five

"Hey, how come you never invited me out for wings and beer before?" said Geoffry as he dug into the pile of wings in front of him.

"Well, you being my big brother, I didn't know I was allowed," Darren joked.

The two men were sitting at the far corner of the bar at Chickie & Pete's, a popular South Philadelphia sports bar not far from Angelo Barbieri's salvage warehouse. Darren had suggested they sit at the bar so as to have a better view of the 76ers game on the wide-screen TV above the bar. But in truth Darren figured that sitting at the bar would help create the chummy feel he was going for while letting him avoid looking directly at Geoffry's shit-eating grin.

"Long as you're paying you can invite me anytime you want, little Bro," said Geoffry through a mouthful of chicken. He took a swig of the tall beer he'd ordered then continued, "Hey, remember that time you were in high school and you couldn't find that English paper you wrote?"

"It was a History paper, but yeah, I remember that."

"You remember where it finally turned up?"

"Yeah."

"How Mom found it under the couch like a week later?"

"Yeah." *Yeah, and I knew it was you who stole it out of my backpack and put it there, you prick!*

"And how everybody thought you were such a dick to lose your paper under the couch and Mom cracked your nuts about it 'til you cried like a pussy?"

"Yeah." *I cried because I was fifteen years old and my wicked step-mother refused to believe that her useless twenty-one-year-old college drop-out son would do such a fucked-up thing and I wanted to punch you both out but couldn't.*

"You ever figure out how that English paper got there?"

"Nope." *It was a history paper and of course I figured it out, you idiot!*

"It was, huh, huh, huh, *me!*" Geoffry laughed as if his sides would split while Darren laughed as hard as he could force himself. *Oh, I'm so doing this, you clown. Just give me one little opening.*

"Well," said Geoffry, wiping his eyes with his sleeve, "I figure I probably shouldn't of done that, I mean it was a jerk move."

One among many jerk moves, you jerk, Darren silently answered.

"But then you were such a little wuss back then, it was so easy to set you off, I never could resist."

"Yeah, well...we were just kids." *I was just a kid. You were a twisted case of arrested development.*

"But, hey, didn't I make it all up to you?" said Geoffry, who'd by now recovered from his laughing fit.

"Oh, yeah?"

"Well, yeah...I mean, look how I got you all set up with Angelo. You'd of been up shit creek if I hadn't."

"You think?"

"According to Mom."

"Mom told you I was up shit creek? She actually said 'shit creek?'"

"Nah, she didn't say 'shit creek' exactly. I don't remember what she said. But that's what she meant."

"Huh," said Darren. *Just give me an opening,* thought Darren, *Just one little opening.*

"So I figure you owe me," said Geoffry, "for setting you up with Angelo like I did."

The light of inspiration flashed in Darren's brain. *And there's my opening,* he thought. "Oh, yeah," he said to his step-brother, "I owe you big time for getting me in with Angelo."

"Even though he likes to break your balls?" snickered Geoffry. "Hey, how do you put up with Angelo breaking your balls all the time?"

Ah, Bro, you are making this too easy, thought Darren. "Eh, all the money he's paying me I can afford to buy myself a new pair."

Geoffry laughed then stopped. "What, Angelo's paying you a lot of money?"

"Oh yeah. An ass load. I'm having trouble spending all the money he's throwing at me."

"Angelo's throwing money at you?"

"By the ass load."

"You shitting me?"

"I shit you not."

"Like how *much* money?"

"I've been working for Barbieri for, what, about six months now? I've already pocketed…" *oh, what the hell,* Darren thought. He leaned in close to Geoffry and lowered his voice to just above a whisper, "…almost *three-quarters of a million.*"

"The fuck you did! For what?" shouted Geoffry, so that people sitting down the bar from him looked over and frowned.

"Shhh, keep it down, Bro," whispered Darren. The he added, "For, you know, flipping a couple of houses."

"Ah, no, fuckin' way he paid you that much for flipping a couple of houses," Geoffry said in a lowered voice.

"Okay, don't go spreading it all around," said Darren, "you know Angelo doesn't like his business spread all around. But maybe I do a couple other little things."

"You do?" Geoffry asked incredulously, "for Barbieri?"

"Maybe. Just a couple little things. Here and there. Now and then."

"Like *what?"*

Darren chuckled. "Like letting him bust my balls. But hey, you know Barbieri only does that when he has an audience. Like when you're there, or somebody. Otherwise he's very respectful to me. Very respectful. As I'm sure he is to you, too."

"Yeah. Barbieri respects me. A lot."

"That's what I figured. Like, he only calls you a dumb-assed oobatz and a dick-for-brains in front of other people."

"What are you talking about? He never called me that shit!"

"Well, that's what I mean, not to your *face*. Just when he's trying to show off. Like when you're not around and he's got an audience, you know, like me or whoever. He'll say things like, 'Don't be a plank like that assface Geoffry,' and then he expects me and everybody else to laugh, and all. I don't like it myself, and I figure he ranks me down behind my back just as much, right? But what can we do, you and me? It's just Angelo being Angelo. Hey, all the money he's paying us, we put up with it, right? I mean, I can't even imagine what he must be paying *you*, you being his right-hand man, and all."

"Yeah," Geoffry said bitterly, "he pays me great." Then he attacked the remains of his wings in silence, polished off his beer and ordered another. "You're paying," he snapped at his step-brother.

"Yeah, I'm paying," Darren replied and he thought, *and so are you, my asshole Bro, so are you.*

Chapter Six

It occurred to Dr. Laura Cavanni that Trysta looked tired and irritable as she lifted Miri from her carrier and settled the baby onto her lap. "How's little Miri doing today?" Dr. Cavanni decided to ask, since asking a mother about her baby was generally as good a conversation-starter as any.

Trysta immediately burst into tears. "Nobody loves me," she wailed, "I'm going to end up alone and broke, living with my parents and trying to support a baby on my own with a waitress job!"

Dr. Cavanni closed her eyes for a moment and tilted her head slightly, trying to process what she'd just heard. "Wait...Why do you think that nobody loves you? Or that you're going to end up broke? Or that you'll have to support your baby on your own? And why with a waitress job?"

"A waitress job in a ritzy restaurant," she sobbed, "you know, where rich guys go for expensive business lunches. And dinners. With lots of drinks."

"Ah," said Dr. Cavanni. She picked up the box of tissues sitting on the floor next to her and offered the box to Trysta. "I understand that your situation is a bit, um, *convoluted* at this moment. But tell me why you're so sure that Darren is going to leave you?"

Trysta pulled out several tissues, wiped her eyes and blew her nose. "Because I know how men are. I'm not stupid."

"Stupid? You're one of the most strategic women I've ever known."

"I am?"

"Absolutely. And I'm not disputing what you're telling me. I'd just like to know *why* you believe Darren is about to leave you after he just married you."

"He doesn't love me. I don't think he ever did. My children are driving him crazy. To tell you the truth, they're driving me crazy." In a small voice she asked, "Do you think I'm an awful mother?"

Dr. Cavanni laughed. "'Cause your kids are driving you crazy? Whose kids don't drive them crazy sometimes? God knows mine did. And still do."

Trysta's eyes widened. "You have *children?*"

"Yes, I have two sons, aged twenty-one and nineteen. And a granddaughter who just turned one."

"You have a *grand*daughter?"

"I do. My oldest son's daughter." Laura reached for the phone sitting on her desk and began scrolling down. "Here," she said, showing Trysta a photo of a beautiful young black woman holding a chubby biracial baby girl in a frilly pink dress with a matching pink bow in her curly black hair. The baby had her grandmother's deep-set, dark brown almond-shaped eyes.

"Oh," Trysta gasped, looking up at Dr. Cavanni, "she's..."

"Beautiful, isn't she?" Laura smiled affectionately. "That's my baby girl."

Trysta studied the photo. "How old is her mother?"

"She's also twenty-one," said Dr. Cavanni.

"Just like me," Trysta sighed, handing the phone back to Dr. Cavanni.

"Just like you how?" Dr. Cavanni asked, setting her phone back on her desk.

"I mean, I had Zach when I was nineteen. That's why I married Silvio. Did your son marry her?"

"No," said Dr. Cavanni. "He's in college. At Temple."

"Oh. What about her? His...girlfriend?"

"She's also taking classes. At Chestnut Hill. Though my son isn't dating her anymore."

"He's not? Why not?"

Dr. Cavanni raised her eyebrows and looked towards the ceiling. "I'm afraid none of this has been my darling son's finest moment." She sighed. "I'm sure he was just toying with this girl, though I know she wasn't toying with him."

"That's just like me, too. I *know* Jeremy was just toying with me."

"Jeremy?"

"Oh, I meant, um…Silvio. I mean, Darren." Trysta turned red and began nervously running a hand through her hair.

"But didn't both Silvio and Darren marry you? Trysta? Who's Jeremy?"

Trysta didn't answer for a moment, then she snapped, "I don't want to talk about it."

Dr. Cavanni, though she was eager to discover what she thought might be a major piece to the puzzle of this woman's life, simply shrugged and said, "Okay."

Then Trysta said, "Jeremy is…I mean, he *probably* is…"

Laura waited, her eyes fixed on Trysta.

"I mean, Jeremy is probably Miri's father."

"Oh," said Dr. Cavanni.

"And Zach's father was Jeremy, too."

"*Oh*," said Dr. Cavanni. "So…Jeremy is…a lover? Possibly both Zach's and Miri's father?"

"Well, not exact…you're not going to tell anybody this, right?"

"No. I'm not." *Who'd believe it?*

"Because I really shouldn't be telling *anybody* this."

No shit, thought Laura, now chomping at the bit to know what it was that this woman shouldn't be telling anyone. She kept her eyes fixed on Trysta to let her know she was still listening. *Talk to me,* she said silently, *talk to me.*

"I mean, I *haven't* told anybody. But I can tell you, right?"

"Of course you can, Trysta." *That's it, keep talking.*

Trysta sighed and shifted the baby in her lap. "See, there were two Jeremys."

"Two Jeremys?" *Two Jeremys? How much crazier does this get?*

"In my life. There was Jeremy DeCiccio in high school. I was in love with him. But Silvio was in love with me. I got pregnant from Jeremy.

He told me to go get an abortion, and after I let him do *anything* he wanted with me, *anything*. Because I *loved* him." Trysta laughed bitterly. "As if I had any money for an abortion. And my father would have *killed* me. And probably him, too. So anyway, I, um, slept with Silvio. He was a nice guy. I figured he'd be a gentleman and pay for an abortion when I told him I was pregnant. But he actually wanted to *marry* me, can you imagine that?" Trysta smiled at the memory. "So that's why I married Silvio. I *had* to."

Dr. Cavanni nodded. "And what about the second Jeremy?"

"Oh, *him*." Trysta rubbed a sleeve across her eyes. "Jeremy Andrews. He's a really important high-up executive at Highland and Erskerberg, where Darren works now and where I used to work. As a receptionist. He seduced me. Told me that he loved me. Then he dumped when I told him I was expecting. Jeremy Andrews is the cause of all my troubles. If not for him I'd still be married to Silvio."

"How so?" Dr. Cavanni again offered Trysta the tissues. "Here, keep the box by you. Did Silvio find out about Jeremy Andrews? Is that why you and Silvio divorced?"

Trysta pulled out another tissue and wiped her eyes. "Well, no. It's just that…I was so *upset* about being pregnant and Jeremy abandoning me. So when Darren started flirting…he'd just been promoted to Vice-President of, of, Strategic Acquisitions. Not as high up yet and not as rich as Jeremy Andrews, but he was going places in the company. Or so I thought, dumb me."

"So you and Darren…?"

"Look, is it so bad that I wanted something better? I'd been married since I was eighteen, a plumber's wife, working, three children. I just wanted something *better*." Trysta sighed. "I started sleeping with Darren. Then after a few weeks – I had to work fast, of course – I told him I was pregnant and that the baby was his and he bought it. Most guys are so clueless about being pregnant."

Dr. Cavanni chuckled. "I expect that's because they've never been."

"Right? They have all the fun and then we get stuck with the babies. But I *love* my babies," Trysta added defensively.

"Of course you do. But tell me…do you not find sex…fun? At least sometimes?"

46

Trysta shrugged. "I mean, maybe sometimes. Or least I think it used to be. Sometimes. I can't really remember. Now it's mostly just work. One more chore at the end of the day before I can go to sleep for a few hours before she wakes up." Trysta shifted Miri from her lap to her shoulder.

"But you say you think sex used to be fun sometimes?"

"Maybe sometimes, I guess. It's always fun getting someone to fall in love with you."

"And sex was the way to get a man or a boy to fall in love with you?"

Trysta's eyes widened with incredulity at the question. "How else do you get them to love you? Or keep loving you?"

"Hmmm," said Dr. Cavanni. She unclipped the pen from the small notepad sitting in her lap and stopped to take a few notes. "So then," she continued, "you told Darren that you were pregnant and that the baby was his and he believed you."

"Yes. I told him that I hadn't slept with Silvio since I'd been with him or for a long time before that. That was sort of true. At least the part about not sleeping with Silvio once I started sleeping with Darren. Well, maybe that wasn't exactly true, either. But I was already pregnant when I started sleeping with Darren. So Miri couldn't be Darren's." Trysta shrugged. "I guess she could be Silvio's."

"Trysta, Silvio is not the father of Miri."

"Well, he's probably not," Trysta moved on, missing the opening Laura was trying to offer her. "I tried not to sleep with him when I was with Jeremy. I wanted the baby to be Jeremy's."

Laura paused again. "You wanted the baby to be Jeremy's?"

"When I got pregnant. Which I figured I would. And I did."

"Trysta, if I may ask…have you *ever* been on birth control?"

"Of course. I'm on the pill now. I've *been* on the pill. Most of the time. I mean most of the time since I was married. Not when I was in high school, though. I should have been. When I was in high school, I mean. But I didn't know where to get it from. My father would have killed me if he ever found out I was on the pill. I mean, before I was married."

"Oh," said Dr. Cavanni. "But then…why did you figure you'd get pregnant with Jeremy – the second Jeremy – if you were on the pill?"

"Well…I can tell you this, right?"

"Of course."

Trysta hesitated. "I stopped taking the pill when I was sleeping with Jeremy Andrews. I thought – dumb me – that Jeremy liked me...*loved* me...and that if I were having his baby..."

"That he would want to marry you."

Trysta began crying again. "He told me to get an abortion, and, and, *dropped* me, just like the other Jeremy. But then Darren came along, so I figured..."

"Right," Laura finished for her.

"But then Jeremy got Darren fired..."

"What?" Dr. Cavanni exclaimed in spite of herself, "Jeremy got Darren *fired*?"

"Of *course* he did," Trysta sniffed, "I'm sure Jeremy was behind it. But Darren has no idea. I don't know what reason they gave him for firing him, but *I* know that's why. Jeremy did it after Darren married me and I quit my job to have the baby and be a stay at home mom. And if I hadn't quit I'm sure Jeremy would have found some way to get me fired. See," Trysta said sadly, "it was really *me* Jeremy was trying to get rid of. And so of course he'd make sure I never got hired back to my old job at Highland and Erskerberg."

Trysta began another round of crying. Laura offered her more tissues, patiently waiting until she'd cried herself out, speaking in the tone she often used to calm distraught animals and patients. "It's all right. It's all right."

"I wish you were my mother," Trysta said.

"Why do you wish I was your mother?" Laura asked, sensing that they were about to get to what her father would call the meat and potatoes.

"Because you wouldn't have kicked me out for getting pregnant. And you wouldn't have let my father kick me out, either."

Laura Cavanni smiled. "No. But again I remind you, I'm not your mother. Or your father."

"I wouldn't have had to get married right away. I'd probably have gone to college, or community college, or something. I could have been something. I'm not as dumb as everybody thinks."

"Trysta...why do people think you're dumb?"

"Because I let them. They expect it, you know?"

"Who expects it?"

"Men. They're the only ones who count, really."

"Good Lord, Trysta, how in the world…" *could you think such a thing,* she wanted to say; but it was perfectly clear to Laura Cavanni how a woman like Trysta could, in fact, think such a thing. How that way of thinking more or less defined Trysta's reality. Instead Dr. Cavanni said, "We've got to get you out of that way of thinking. Trysta, *you're* the one who counts, don't you see?"

"I am?"

"Of course you are. You are a beautiful, intelligent, and quite frankly, savvy woman."

"I am?"

"Yes, you are."

"Really?"

"Really."

Trysta teared up again.

"But you've got to stop crying." Dr. Cavanni sighed. "Here," she said gently, once more handing Trysta the tissues.

"It's just that," Trysta sniffed, "nobody's ever told me I was intelligent before. Or savvy. Or beautiful unless they wanted, you know, sex, or something, from me."

"You do know that you're beautiful."

"Yes." For all the times she'd heard those words, used as barter in exchange for sexual favors, favors which Trysta would then dole out as barter of her own, she felt as though she were hearing them for the first time.

"And smart."

"Yes." Trysta felt as if some desert patch of her soul was blooming to life from a sweet, refreshing rain. "Yes," she softly repeated. She raised her eyes and felt as if she were being drawn into those deep, dark, beautiful almond eyes still fixed on her.

"Good," said Dr. Cavanni, smiling at Trysta in a way that made Trysta's cheeks flush and her heart flutter. "You did well again today, Trysta. Now, if we're going to continue our sessions,"

"I'd like that," Trysta said shyly.

"So would I," said Dr. Cavanni and Trysta blushed again. "Tell me, do you have an insurance card I could take a look at?"

"Yes, yes, I..." Trysta, in her haste, clumsily shifted little Miri and fumbled for her purse then her wallet for her insurance card which she handed to Dr. Cavanni with a slightly trembling hand.

Dr. Cavanni studied the card for a moment then said, "Yep, this is a good one. Give me a minute." Dr. Cavanni returned to her desk, flipped open her laptop and made a few entries. "You'll have a thirty-dollar co-pay which I could bill you for later. That work?"

Trysta smiled and nodded.

Dr. Cavanni made a few more entries then returned Trysta's card, touching Trysta's fingers ever so briefly, but to Trysta the touch felt electric. "So shall we meet next week, same time, same place?"

"Yes," Trysta said happily, "yes."

"Okay, well, in the meantime I want you to think about something else: What is it you really want for your life? Because, see, the great challenge is not so much getting what you want as figuring out what it is you want. So think about that, okay? And next time we can maybe talk about what you want and how you might possibly make it happen."

"Oh, *thank* you, Dr. Cavannni. Thank you *so much!*"

Dr. Cavanni smiled and accompanied Trysta to the door of her office. After Trysta left, Laura leaned her back against the closed door. "*Oh* boy," she muttered and wondered if she'd just made a big mistake.

***

Later that night Trysta donned her sexiest negligee and for the first time in a well over a week came to Darren's side of the bed and made such sweet, passionate love to him that afterwards, as he lay back in a state of drowsy, post-coital satisfaction, he half-considered hanging on to her and maybe even the baby, for whom he'd been keeping an ear open while they made love – she'd been a little fussy before he put her down this evening – if Silvio didn't follow up on the paternity test, which he hadn't so far. Darren yawned and his last thought before drifting off was that they'd definitely have to change her name to Miri. Just Miri. Miri Miller.

Trysta, too, lay in a state of physical satisfaction, bliss, really, as she closed her eyes and continued the fantasy she'd just played out with her body and in her mind, imagining that the arms that had just held her and the lips that had just kissed her and the body that had just thrilled her body were not those of the man lying next to her, but of her new love. Her true love.

Dr. Cavanni, she thought. "Laura," she whispered oh-so-softly, trying out the sound of the name on her lips.

Trysta smiled. She knew what – who – it was that she wanted.

Chapter Seven

Silvio was distracted. Sally could tell by the way he sat on her sofa, absently scrolling through his phone, holding up his end of the conversation but minimally, physically next to her but mentally across town. He'd been distracted for days. It was annoying.

At least he'd come by after work this night, had eaten some supper, spent a little time with Josh and David before Sally put them to bed. Sometimes he stayed at Quick and Reliable so late that he didn't stop by. Well, that wasn't really all that abnormal, sometimes Silvio did work too late to come by even before all this stuff with Trysta's baby. Except that these days Sally wondered if he was staying late working or ruminating.

Trysta. God, would Sally ever be free of that woman in her life? Not likely. No more likely than Silvio ever being free of Darren. Except that Darren didn't seem to bug Silvio anymore as much as Trysta bugged Sally. Probably because Darren wasn't sucking up Sally's attention the way Trysta was sucking up Silvio's these days.

Trysta and her baby. That's all they talked about. All talk and no action. Because Silvio didn't know what he wanted to do about the baby who might or might not be his. He could hardly wrap his head around it. He couldn't even bring himself to get the damn paternity test.

What if Silvia was his, he'd wonder; how could he take a nursing baby away from her mother? He didn't really know the baby, the baby didn't know him. Should he get into another drawn-out legal fight with Trysta over a baby he didn't even know? Was that even fair?

"Silvio," Sally would say, "don't sweat the details yet, just go get the test first, find out if the baby's yours."

"But what if she's not?" Silvio would invariably come back.

"Then problem solved," Sally would reply, knowing what the next issue would be.

"But," he'd come back after thinking up some excuse, "how will it be for my other kids if I take them away from their baby sister? The little girls keep asking me if Silvia is gonna come when they come to live with me. They want her to come, too. What'll I do if she's not mine?"

"I don't know, go talk to Charleston Tilley," Sally would tell him, "maybe you guys could work out some visitation thing with Trysta, or something. But look, Silvio, you're not even *there* yet," Sally had said more times than she could count, "*first* you've gotta decide what you want to do if it turns out that she's yours, *second* you've gotta decide what you want to do if she *isn't* yours, and *third* you've gotta find out whether she is or isn't yours, and then *fourth*, you've gotta follow through on what you decided you wanted to do when you found out whether she's yours or not. It's like Mr. Tilley said, right?"

And 'round and 'round they'd go, getting nowhere because Silvio seemed paralyzed by all the worry, emotion, and indecision that could grip the mind and heart of a person in the middle of a custody battle, especially one that had taken such a crazy turn as this one had.

Well, hell, it wasn't as if Sally hadn't known what she was signing onto when she'd hitched her horse to Silvio's wagon. *Hitched my horse to Silvio's wagon? Did I just think that? Holy crap, am I channeling my mother now?*

"What are you laughing at?" Silvio asked, looking up from his phone.

"Oh, nothing," said Sally, feeling a little better because Silvio had noticed that she'd been chuckling to herself, "it's just that I'm starting to sound like my mother."

Silvio laughed. "You haven't said anything."

"I was sounding like my mother in my head."

"What was your mother saying in your head?"

"That I hitched my horse to your wagon."

"What?" Silvio laughed again.

"It means when someone is connected to your life then you're connected to theirs, too."

"That's what you were thinking?"

"Yeah."

"That's nice." Silvio put down his phone, wrapped his arm around Sally's shoulder and kissed her cheek.

"Silvio, are we still engaged?" Sally blurted.

"What?" Silvio's smile faded and his eyes widened in astonishment. "Well, yeah, of course we're still engaged, why would you ask me that?"

"Well, it's just that we never, you know, talk about it, or anything…" *And you haven't bought me a ring yet,* she thought.

"Aw, Sally, you know how it's been, I mean all that's been going on with the baby, and all."

And here we go again, thought Sally. "Silvio," she said, "*nothing's* been going on with the baby. I mean, all we ever talk about anymore is what to do about the baby. But then you…we…can't decide. Look, how about we just *decide* what you want to do and then do it."

Silvio sighed. "I don't know. I just don't know. I mean, taking her away from her mother? She's so young, and all."

"Fine, then let it go," Sally said, trying to sound gentle. "You'll get your kids, let Silvia stay with her mother, and forget about it. You don't have to do anything. Forget about Darren's paternity test and let's just get on with our lives."

"How can I just forget about it?" said Silvio, raising his voice. "If Silvia's mine I'm supposed to just forget about her?"

"So fine, let's go back to Charleston, tell him you want the paternity test. Then if she's yours and you want custody, or part custody, or whatever, we go back to Charleston and work it out."

"Yeah, and what if I go through all the trouble, get Trysta all stirred up, and all, and the baby's not even mine?"

"Trysta?" Sally sprung up. "You're worried about Trysta? Is that what this is about?"

Now Silvio sprung up so that they stood face-to-face. "Oh, come on, Sally, you know it's not!"

"No? Well, I don't know what it's about! I mean, all you have to do is make up your mind, then we go back and see Charleston and get the damn test! What's so freakin' hard about that?"

"And every time *we* go back and see Charleston it's costing *me* money!"

Sally threw up her hands. *"Costing you money?*What the hell do you care how much money it's costing you? Look, Silvio, you work like a dog, since you took over your uncle's business you've had money falling out your butthole, what the hell else do you wanna spend your money on?"

"What, now you're *cursing* at me?"

"Aw, come on, Silvio, I'm not"

"Mommy! Mommy!"

"Joshua!" Sally and Silvio gasped together. They both hurried towards the sound of the crying coming from Joshua's bedroom, Sally taking a detour towards the crying that was now coming from baby David's room.

While Sally picked up David and tried to bounce him back to sleep Silvio sat on the edge of Joshua's bed. "Hey, what's wrong? Bad dream?"

Joshua crawled onto Silvio's lap. "Wh-where's M-Mommy?" he sobbed breathlessly.

"Your brother decided to wake up, too, so she's getting him. And I'm getting you."

"I don't want you and Mommy to fight," he cried.

"Fight?" Silvio chuckled, his heart stabbed with a pang of guilt, "You think your Mom and I were *fighting?"*

Josh nodded.

"What, you thought Silvio and I were *fighting?"* Sally chuckled as she entered Josh's room carrying now wide-awake David, "No, no we weren't *fighting."*

"I heard you fighting," Josh sobbed, "and I don't *want* you to fight!"

"Aw, we weren't fighting with each other," Silvio lied, "we were just talking about, uh, the news, how the price of milk is going up and we don't think it should. Right, Mommy?"

"Right." Sally sat next to Silvio on the bed holding David in her lap. "We just got a little mad because the price of milk is going up. But it's okay."

"Will I still be able to have my milk?" Joshua asked, his eyes wide with concern.

"Oh, sure you will, guy," said Silvio. "It didn't go up that much. Just, like, a nickel. And besides, we got plenty of money. So don't worry about it, okay?"

Silvio tucked Joshua back into his bed and he and Sally kissed him good night.

"Do you guys still love each other?" Josh asked as Silvio, Sally, and David headed for the door.

Sally and Silvio looked at each other. Silvio wrapped his arms around Sally and David. "We love each other so much," he said.

"We do," said Sally, looking into Silvio's eyes.

"Then don't yell about milk anymore."

"We won't. We promise," said Sally.

"We promise," said Silvio.

Josh rolled over to go back to sleep and Sally and Silvio stepped outside his room.

Silvio quietly shut the door. "I'm sorry," he said.

"I'm sorry, too," said Sally. "Let's not argue about the price of milk anymore."

***

Joanne Ponticello was the floor manager at the Northeast Philadelphia accounting firm Zarnecki and Young and Sally Miller's boss. And though in truth Sally thought of Joanne as more of a friend, confidante or even a second mother, Joanne had on more than one occasion tongue-in-cheekily reminded Sally, "Hey, Girl, I'm not your mother; your mother's your mother and I'm your mother's best friend and your boss, got that?"

Sally knew this was true. Joanne had been her mother's best friend as far back as Sally could remember, and it was Joanne who got Sally a low-rung part-time office assistant's job at Zarnecki and Young years ago, back when Sally was in high school. It was likewise Joanne who had pushed Sally to return to college to earn her degree, Sally having dropped out after one year at Philadelphia Community – foolishly, Sally now realized – to marry Darren, have their son Joshua, and stay on at Zarnecki and Young as a full-time, though still low-rung, administrative assistant. And Joanne continued to cheer Sally on in those moments when Sally wondered how she'd ever manage to finish an undergraduate degree, let alone pursue her ultimate dream of a law degree.

Sally sometimes wondered what formed the bond between this boisterous, outspoken, Italian lady and her own straight-laced, uber-religious mother. In truth there were things she felt more comfortable discussing with her boss than her mother, more recent developments in her relationship with Silvio being among them.

"So it wasn't exactly a knock-down-drag-out between you and Silvio," said Joanne after Sally had filled her in on the events from the night before while they sipped coffee-machine lattes in the break room.

"Well, no, but it could have been if we hadn't woken up Josh and David with our yelling."

"You were *yelling*?"

"Oh, not exactly *yelling* yelling. But, you know, my condo is pretty small and the walls are kind of thin and the noise carries."

"Huh, if you and Silvio are gonna be fighting you better get a bigger place," Joanne joked.

"Actually, that's sort of related to why I was so upset with Silvio."

Joanne took a sip of her coffee. "Why *were* you so upset with Silvio?"

Sally sighed. "The night this all started, I mean the night Silvio got the call from Darren telling him that Darren's paternity test for Silvia came back negative..."

"Yeah, you told me about that night. The night that will live in infamy."

"Right. Among other nights. Anyway," Sally continued, "what I didn't tell you about that night is that..." Sally paused for a moment and wrapped her hands around her coffee cup. "...Silvio proposed to me."

Joanne's face lit up. "Proposed? Like, *marriage*?"

Sally smiled and nodded.

"*Gurrrrl!* Come on, let me give you a hug!"

The women stood and hugged, then Joanne reached for Sally's hand. "So where's the ring, Girlfriend?"

Sally sighed again and sat back down at the table, as did Joanne. "That's part of the problem."

"Guy proposes to you without a ring? Uh, yeah, I'd say that's a *big* part of the problem."

"No, the problem isn't that he didn't give me a ring the night he proposed. I mean, it was kind of spur of the moment, unplanned, it just kind of happened, you know what I mean?"

"Well, okay, I guess those kind of things do sometimes happen. So go on."

"In fact, it was kind of sweet." Sally smiled at the memory. "Silvio came by and brought me a little cake, I mean, a really beautiful fancy little cake in a box all tied up with a ribbon, just to celebrate that I got an "A" in my first college class."

"Aw, that was sweet."

"I was rocking David to sleep, I was dead tired, we both were, and then he just spontaneously got down on one knee in front of the rocking chair, offered me the cake, and asked me to marry him. I said yes, of course."

"That is really beautiful. And it's *so* Silvio."

"I know." Sally teared up at the memory. "And he was so excited, he wanted to get married right away, and talked about buying a big house for us all, Josh and David and me and him and his kids. He was so happy that night. *I* was so happy." Sally rubbed the back of her hand across her eyes. "And then a few minutes later came the phone call from Darren. And Silvio hasn't brought up getting married right away or buying us a house since."

"Hence you have to do your fighting in a small place with thin walls."

Sally chuckled through her tears. "Yeah. And I guess he sort of forgot about buying me a ring, too."

"Oh, that aggression will not stand, Hon. You tell our guy Silvio he better get a ring on your finger pronto. And one with a nice big rock for all the grief he's been putting you through."

Sally sniffled. "I don't want to ask him. I want him to just, you know, *give* it to me."

Joanne sighed. "Yeah. It's like that line from that movie about that girl who lived in the woods, 'Don't ask for what should be offered.'"

"Well, I never saw the movie about the girl in the woods, but, yeah, that's how I feel. Except that...okay, what's bothering me most of all is that I just can't lose the feeling that this is really all about Trysta. I mean, she's been trying to mess with Silvio's mind ever since the baby was born. Now she's done it."

Joanne reached across the table and took Sally's hand. "Aw, come on, Hon, you know Silvio loves you, not her."

"I know, I know. Except that I think this business about the paternity test is really getting to him. I think just the thought of having to go through it is kind of humiliating for him."

"No kidding. I mean, you're basically asking the guy to take a test to find out if his wife was cheating on him with one guy or two. That would be enough to make any guy go limp."

Sally laughed through her tears then her expression turned serious. "Yeah. We've had that, too."

"*That?*" Joanne asked.

Sally nodded. "Yeah. That."

"Boy, this is *really* getting to him."

Sally sighed. "He wants to find out. But he doesn't. And he can't decide what he'd do if he *did* find out. He can't decide anything because he's stuck back at square A over the stupid paternity test."

"So...All this aside, how does Silvio feel about this baby? I mean he's seen her often enough, right?"

"Well, yeah, sure. I told you about how when he goes to pick up his kids Trysta trots out little Silvia. How Trysta's been trying to make a play for Silvio, trying to get him back ever since she found out that he inherited his uncle's business."

Joanne shook her head. "How trashy can you get?"

"Right?" said Sally.

"And Darren feels *how* about his wife going after her ex-husband?"

"Oh, who the hell knows? He seems pretty anxious to get rid of Trysta's kids, that's for sure. Even though a couple of times when he brought Josh back home after his visitation he brought all Trysta's kids along for the ride, including little Silvia all bundled up and strapped in her car seat." Sally sighed. "She's sure a cute little baby, I'll say that much."

"Silvia is?" Joanne raised her coffee cup and took a sip.

"Oh, yeah. A little blondie, with big dark brown eyes. Cute as a button."

Joanne sputtered on her coffee.

"You okay?" Sally asked. "Did it go down the wrong pipe?"

"Wait," said Joanne, recovering from her coffee, "did you just say Silvia has *dark brown eyes*? Are you *sure*?"

"Yeah, I'm sure. Big, pretty brown eyes. Actually she doesn't look anything like Silvio."

"That's because Silvio isn't her daddy."

Sally drew back in surprise. "What? How do you know?"

"What color are Silvio's eyes?"

"Blue."

"What color are Trysta's eyes?"

"Blue."

"Oh, come on, Sally, didn't you take biology in high school?"

"Yeah?"

"Did you pay attention in class?"

Sally shrugged. "No."

Joanne sighed. "How do I explain this?" She grabbed a napkin. "You have pen on you?"

"No," said Sally.

"Nobody has a pen anymore." Joanne rummaged through her purse. "Here, I have one. Look," she said, "it's genetics. *High school* genetics. Now this time pay attention. Eye color involves a set of two alla..alla..something or others."

"What?"

"These two...*things*...genetic things. They're called alla-something or others."

"Whatever you say."

"As you'd know if you'd of been paying attention in high school biology class."

"Aw, c'mon, Joanne," Sally laughed, "gimme a break."

"Anyway," Joanne wrote a capital "B" on the napkin, "the big B's are dominant, they're the alla-thing for brown eyes," she then wrote a small "b," "and these small b's are the alla-thing for blue eyes. They're recessive. Is this ringing a bell at all?"

"All right, yeah, kind of."

"Okay, dominant domineers recessive. Remember that. Every eye gets two alla-things to give it color. Now, say somebody with two big B's – a brown-eyed person," Joanne wrote two capital B's on the napkin, "marries somebody with two little b's,"

"A blue-eyed person," Sally finished for her.

"Correct," said Joanne, writing two small b's. "Their kid will be this," She drew a capital B next to a small b, "and will have brown eyes because"

"Dominant domineers recessive," Sally finished for her.

"Right," said Joanne, writing and connecting big B's and little b's as she spoke. "But if two big B-little-b's marry, then their kids could be a big-B-little-b brown-eyed, or"

"…two little b blue-eyeds," Sally finished for her.

"Right," said Joanne. "But if two little b blue-eyeds have a kid,"

"…the kid can only have blue eyes because there are no big B's in the mix." Sally sighed. "Yeah, I get it. Trysta and Silvio could only have a blue-eyed baby."

"Don't shoot the messenger, okay?" said Joanne, again patting Sally's hand.

"No, no, I'm glad you told me, Joanne. Thanks. I guess." They sat for a few moments in silence. "I sure wish Silvio and I had paid attention in biology class. It would have made this thing a whole lot simpler."

"Not mention that you'd probably have your ring by now."

"Yeah," said Sally, wiping away a rogue tear.

***

"So you see how it is?" Sally asked gently, setting a cup of coffee and a slice of cake before Silvio. "There's these two alleles. That make the eye color."

"Yeah," said Silvio, still gazing at Sally's laptop, studying the article in the *Science Daily* website entitled, "Blue Eyes, A Clue to Paternity," one of three articles she'd pulled up for him on the subject.

"So now you don't have to take any test. I mean, now we know, right?"

"Yeah, I guess." Silvio ate a few bites of cake without much enthusiasm.

"So what's wrong?" asked Sally. "You're not the baby's father. We can go back to where we were before this whole thing started."

"I can't." Silvio shook his head. "I can't. I mean, ever since we got that phone call it's all I've been thinking about it."

"Yeah, I know," Sally sighed.

"I can't just suddenly stop thinking about it." Silvio wrapped his hands around his coffee mug. "I'd rather I was the father. Then at least I'd know what I had to do." Silvio stood up and began pacing. "Geeze, how many men was Trysta sleeping with?"

"So this is about Trysta?"

"No, it's about this little girl who's my kids' sister but the guy who's supposed to be her father isn't."

So don't snap at me, Sally thought, holding her tongue, grateful that this was Josh's weekend with Darren.

"I mean, even if Silvia's not mine I can't just put her out of my head anymore. Because she's not Darren's either." Silvio began gesturing, throwing his hands into the air. "She's sleeping with me, sleeping with Darren, sleeping with some other guy, other *guys*, who knows how many, and do *any* of them care about this little girl?"

"Silvio," Sally said softy, cocking her head towards the bedroom where David was sleeping, "the baby. I mean," she hinted, "we're not in our nice big house yet with two floors and all the bedrooms."

But Sally's hint passed him by, though he did lower his voice.

"Darren doesn't want her. He doesn't want her any more than he wants my kids."

"Do *you* want Silvia?"

"Do *I* want her?" Silvio stopped pacing a moment, considered, then continued pacing. "I don't know. What difference does it make what I want? Trysta's fighting me on getting custody of my own kids, you think she'd give me custody of one who's not even mine?"

"I wonder if Darren still thinks you're the father. I mean, I wonder if *he's* found out yet that Trysta was sleeping with somebody else besides you and him."

"That's his problem," snapped Silvio.

"Maybe he'll kick her out," said Sally just to be contrary, "then what?"

"Yeah, well, that's *her* problem!" Silvio threw his hands up again. "What am I supposed to do about it?"

"You could start by not yelling at *me*," snapped Sally, "like all this is *my* fault!"

"I'm sorry Sally. It's like this whole thing has just opened this big can of worms in my head. I think I better go."

"What? Why? It's Friday night. I just got the baby down. Don't you want to stay? Look, Josh is at Darren's…Don't you want to stay the night?"

"No, I…I need to think, I need to…" Silvio kissed Sally distractedly on the forehead. "I'm sorry, Sally, I need to go." Then he headed for the door, grabbing his coat from the closet on his way out.

Sally stood by her dinette table, looking at the door. She picked up the plate of Silvio's half-eaten cake. "You didn't finish your cake," she sniffed, putting a forkful of cake into her mouth as a tear rolled down her cheek.

Sally's front door swung open and Silvio hurried back inside. "You wanna know what my problem is?" he asked, hurrying across the living room to where Sally stood at her dinette table.

"Yes," she said through her mouthful of cake, "I do." She wiped her eyes with her sleeve.

"You're crying? Aw, Sally, why are you crying? Are you okay?"

Sally shook her head, swallowed her cake, and burst into sobs.

"What is it? What's wrong?" Silvio reached into his pocket and took out a handkerchief.

"Y-you…don't kn-know?"

"What?" he asked, wiping her eyes, his own his eyes filled with concern, "Because I left you just now?"

"No. Because you left me the night you got that phone call from Darren and you've been gone ever since."

"What do you..." Silvio stopped mid-sentence as Sally's meaning sunk in.

Sally snatched the handkerchief from Silvio's hand and finished wiping her tears. "I want to help you through this. I want to be there for you, I want us to get through this *together*, but you've been shutting me out, like there's no room for me anymore in all the confusion about the baby and Trysta and, and *everything!* Don't you see, Silvio? What we had, we're losing it. And I don't know how to hold on to it by myself."

Silvio stood momentarily dumbfounded, as if he'd been struck in the face or hit with cold water.

"Aw geeze Sally...aw geeze." He wrapped his arms around Sally and held her close. "What's wrong with me? What the hell's wrong with me? Did I let this happen again? Did I really let this happen again?"

"Let what happen again?" asked Sally, her head resting against Silvio's chest.

"Let her make me crazy again, and me running around in my head like a wild bull in a"

"China shop," Sally finished the sentence along with him, "Like my mom sometimes says."

"Yeah, that's what my mom says, too, about people who are out of control. Wrecking things. Like I was doing after my divorce, when I was so crazy I wrecked my chances for getting any custody of my kids. And now look at me, acting all crazy again, and almost wrecking..." He began gently stroking her hair. "Aw Sally, I'm so sorry, I didn't mean to leave you. I didn't mean to make you cry."

"I know, I know."

"You okay now?" He asked.

"Yeah, I'm okay." Sally looked up into Silvio's eyes. "But look at you, now you're crying, too." She began wiping his eyes with the handkerchief.

"I love you," he said softly, "even when I'm acting like a dumb jerk."

"I love you, too. And you're not a dumb jerk."

"Yeah, I am. And I'm sorry."

"Oh, it's all right. I know you've been upset over the baby and Trysta sleeping with all those guys, and all."

"Aw what do I even care who Trysta slept with? And I'm gonna stop worrying about her baby, right now. It's her baby. I got my own kids – our kids – and you – to worry about."

"You don't have to worry about me, Silvio," Sally said, a warm feeling rising up inside her. "Are we done crying?" she asked, holding up Silvio's handkerchief, "'Cause I don't want to forget to give you back your hanky."

Silvio chuckled and took back his handkerchief, stuffing it into his pocket. He picked up the plate of cake still sitting on Sally's table. "Here," he said, feeding her a forkful of cake then eating a forkful himself. "Let's finish our cake, forget all our problems, watch some TV, and then go to bed."

"Okay," said Sally. *Thank you, God,* she silently added.

Chapter Eight

"I'm certainly glad to see you boys finally getting along," said Donna Miller, raising her eyebrows at Darren then smiling warmly at her son Geoffry as she placed on the dining room table a woven basket filled with fine-ground sea-salt almond crackers.

"That's because Darren finally stopped acting like an asshole," Geoffry sniggered.

Trina and Sam put their hands over their mouths and squealed, Zach muttered, "Huh," and Josh looked over at Darren, so wounded for his father and fearful that the grown-ups might start fighting that his eyes began to water.

"Uh, Geoffry? The kids?" said Ed Miller, Darren's father and Geoffry's step-father, as he set a tureen of vichyssoise on the table.

Donna chuckled uncomfortably. "Uncle Geoffry's going to have to put a quarter in the swear jar for that. Here, Ed," she said to her husband, "why don't you just walk around the table with the vichyssoise and let everybody help themselves. Of course," she said, looking pointedly at Darren, "Geoffry doesn't normally use that language, so I'm just wondering who he's suddenly picking it up from."

"Probably from this guy we do contract work for," said Darren, ignoring his step-mother's implication. "That guy cusses like a longshoreman."

"Well, so does somebody else we know, right Trysta?"

"Huh?" asked Trysta, who looked up from the soup she'd been absently ladling into her bowl while her thoughts lie elsewhere, far from this Saturday afternoon family lunch at her in-laws' home.

"You're always telling me about Darren's potty mouth problem." Donna looked over at the children sitting around the card table she'd set up for them. "Now you children know not to use that language, right?"

Sam, Trina and Josh nodded. Zach rolled his eyes.

"Joshua's crying," Sam whispered in her sister's ear.

"That's because Uncle Geoffry called his dad a *um-um*," Trina whispered back.

"Are you crying?" Sam whispered to Josh.

Josh shook his head but the question made his eyes water more.

"Hold his hand," Trina whispered into Sam's ear.

Sam took Josh's hand and whispered, "Are you all better now?"

Josh nodded and rubbed his sleeve across his eyes.

"Hey, Josh," Zach said softly, "look." Zach crossed his eyes and lifted the tip of his nose with his fingers to make a pig snout. Josh and the girls laughed.

"Oh, listen to all that laughing," said Donna, smiling. "Aren't they just the happiest children? Ed, give the children some vichyssoise."

Ed set the tureen of soup on the table. But as he filled the ladle Sam put her hand over her bowl. "No! I don't like swishyswaz!"

"Me neither," said Trina, covering her bowl as well.

"*What?*" Donna called over from the grown-ups table, "you don't like vichyssoise?"

"Geeze, you never even tried it," said Zach.

"I don't like the grass in it or the dirt," said Sam.

"Me neither," said Trina.

"*What?*" Donna chuckled, though with an edge in her voice. "Why, those are chives. And herbs. They make it *soooo* good. Ed, give them a little to try."

"*Nooooo!*" the girls cried.

"Fine," huffed Donna, shooting a pointed look at Darren then at Trysta, who seemed overly-focused on her soup.

"Okay," said Ed, holding the ladle suspended in air. "How about you, Josh? You want some…swishyswaz?"

Josh shook his head. "I only like chicken noodle."

"Yeah, chicken noodle!" cried Trina, "We want chicken noodle!"

"Yeah, we want chicken noodle!" echoed Sam.

"We want chicken noodle! We want chicken noodle!" cried Trina and Sam, pounding their spoons on the table.

"Oh, oh, oh," cried Donna, "we don't do that! Darren? Trysta? You need to"

"SHUT UP!" Zach yelled at his sisters, who immediately ceased.

"Shhh, *guys*," said Darren, "you'll wake the baby. She's just down the hall, right?"

"Fine," Zach mumbled.

"Whataya say, Zach?" asked Ed, still holding the ladle full of soup.

"Okay, I'll try some," said Zach, holding up his bowl.

"I'll try some, too," said Josh, holding up his bowl in imitation of his step-brother.

"All *right*," said Ed, ladling a scoop of soup into each bowl. "How old are you now, Josh? Still six?"

"Yes, I'm six but I'll be seven on April ninth."

"Well, we'll have to do something special on your birthday," said Donna.

"Silvio's gonna take me to his shop on my birthday and let me work with him because then I'll be seven."

The adults exchanged looks and even Trysta looked up from her soup at the mention of Silvio's name.

"Oooo, *burn*," Geoffry said quietly behind his hand, smirking and stabbing Darren in the ribs with his elbow. Darren winced in pain then smiled.

"Oh, you two," chuckled Donna, who'd caught Geoffry's assault on Darren.

Ed returned to the grown-up's table and set down the vichyssoise. "Hey, Hon, don't we have a box or two of Lipton's left over from my flu last month?"

"Yes, we do," Donna sighed.

"All right!" Ed called over to the children's table, "So who wants some chicken noodle?"

"Me!" cried Trina, Sam and Josh.

"I guess I'll have some, too," said Zach, putting down his spoonful of vichyssoise.

"Yeah, get me some, too, Ed," said Geoffry, pushing away his bowl.

"Oh, *Geoffry*," Donna chuckled affectionately, reaching across the table to pat her son's hand, "*you're* the biggest kid here!"

"Lucky Grandma loves to spoil you guys so much," said Ed, eying Geoffry for an instant and shaking his head ever so slightly as he headed out to the kitchen.

"Trysta, you've got to teach these children to appreciate good, healthy food and to eat what's put in front of them," said Donna.

"Yes," said Trysta, smiling dreamily, "yes."

After lunch Ed suggested that the men wash the dishes so that the women could go relax and the children go play. Geoffry followed the children into the family room while his mother and Trysta headed for the living room.

Donna settled into one of the leather Barcalounger armchairs by the fireplace. "Can you believe she'd let that man take her son to a filthy, dangerous *plumbing* business? Full of who knows what kind of rough characters, I'm sure."

"Well," Trysta sighed, taking the matching chair across from Donna, "that's Sally for you. There's nothing I can do about it."

"Darren could certainly do something about it," Donna snipped, "Josh is *his* son."

"Oh, *Darren*," said Trysta. "Just try to get him to do *anything* these days."

"Oh, I know, dear, believe me, I know," said Donna, waving the air in a gesture of exasperation.

Trina and Sam came running into the living room from the family room. "Grandma," cried Trina, "you said we could watch 'Minnie Mouse's Boutique' on TV after lunch if we were good and we were good and now Uncle Geoffry won't let us!"

"He's watching fighting and we don't *like* fighting," cried Sam, "and Josh doesn't like fighting, too!"

Josh and Zach followed the girls into the living room, Zach carrying a laptop. "Grandma, can Zach and me play our video game in here?" said Josh, "We don't like the fighting."

"It's called 'boxing,'" said Zach as he flopped down on the couch and flipped open his laptop.

"Yes, you boys may play your video game in here," said Donna.

"But what about us?" cried Trina. "Uncle Geoffry won't let us watch 'Minnie Mouse's Boutique' and you said we could!"

"Yeah, you said we could!" echoed Sam.

"Now, girls," said Donna firmly, "this is Uncle Geoffry's house, and"

"No it's not, Grandma, it's yours!" cried Trina. "Uncle Geoffry doesn't even live here!"

"Yeah, it's yours, Grandma!" cried Sam.

"*Excuse* me, young ladies?" said Donna with an exaggerated frown.

"Hey, what's all the racket out there?" Ed called from the kitchen, "You're gonna wake the baby!"

"Oh, wonderful, Ed," said Donna petulantly, cocking her head towards the bedroom down the hall from the living room, "now *you* woke her."

"*Me?*"

"Have Darren go get her," said Donna, "Trysta and I were talking."

"No, I'll get her," said Trysta, who wanted to get away from the tempest she knew was about to break in the living room.

Trina and Sam began crying. "It's not fair!" They wailed.

Josh began sniffling as well.

"I'm sorry, this is *not* how we behave at Grandma's house," said Donna tersely. "Grandpa," she called to her husband, "Tell these children this is *not* how they"

"What's wrong?" Darren called from the kitchen.

"Hey, could you keep it down out there?" Geoffry called from the family room, "I can't hear the fight!"

"Fine," Zach shouted over the ruckus, "you can watch stupid Minnie Mouse on my laptop. Me and Josh'll get the soccer ball from the car. You want to go outside and play soccer?" Zach asked Josh.

Josh nodded and hopped off the couch, wiping his eyes.

"Put on your coats," Donna called to the boys as they headed for the back door. "And girls, why don't you go listen to your show in one of the bedrooms so the grown-ups can have a little quiet. There now, that's much better. Phew." Donna rested her head against the back of her chair and closed her eyes as the girls skipped off to a bedroom and the boys shut the door behind them.

***

"So how come you and Geoffry are such good pals all of a sudden?" asked Ed Miller as he and his son loaded the dishwasher.

Darren shrugged. "Eh, why not?"

"You know, I'm not exactly buying it," said Ed, "and neither is you mother."

Step-mother, Darren mumbled under his breath.

"So what's going on?"

Darren sighed. "Aw, Dad, it's just too hard to keep fighting. It takes too much energy. It's easier to just…let it all go. Or put up with it, whatever."

"Well, you got that right, son. Let it go. Just do what you have to do to get along."

At that moment Geoffry entered the kitchen. "Sorry to interrupt you ladies," he snickered. He headed to the refrigerator, opened the door, then pulled out a bottle of Schöfferhofer Hefeweizen beer.

"This all you got?" he asked, frowning at the amber-colored bottle in his hand. "Don't you got anything good? Like a Corona, or something?"

"Ask your Mom," said Ed, "she's the one who buys the beer around here."

"She probably bought this faggoty shit for Darren." Geoffry tried twisting off the cap. Grunting and getting nowhere, he said, "What the fuck, it doesn't even twist off! Where the hell's the bottle opener?"

"You know where we keep it." Ed cocked his head. "In that drawer. And you wanna watch the language around the kids, right?"

"Yeah, yeah, don't worry about the kiddies. Hey, grab the opener for me, Bro," he said to Darren.

Darren retrieved the bottle opener from the drawer. "Tell you what, I'll even open it for you."

"All *right*," said Geoffry, handing Darren his bottle.

"How about you grab a towel and help Darren and me with the dishes?" said Ed.

"Nah, I'm watching the fight." Geoffry raised his opened beer bottle to Darren and Ed. "Have fun washing the dishes, ladies."

After Geoffry left the kitchen Darren and his father cleaned up in silence, Ed in the same silence he'd become accustomed to retreating to over the years whenever there was the possibility of him having to take sides in some triangulated conflict among his son, his wife and his wife's son.

Darren's silence, on the other hand, wasn't this time from choking down the Geoffry-and/or-Donna-induced anger, resentment and helplessness he'd been choking down since his childhood. No, this time Darren, as he wiped down his step-mother's kitchen counters and swept her floor, was ruminating over the details of how exactly he'd use his step-brother as a pawn in his plan to cut himself loose from Angelo Barbieri. Of course, his plan could back-fire in half-a-dozen ways, the worst outcome being Barbieri, in his anger over all the money he'd lose if Darren pulled this off right, might throw caution to the wind and…do something…or have something done…something…*physical*…to Darren.

Still, even the best outcome – Barbieri firing both Darren and Geoffry without having them roughed up – might well include a call from Barbieri to Jeremy Andrews, the head of Global Acquisitions at Highland and Erskerberg. Jeremy Andrews, the Great and Powerful. Huh, great and powerful flunky of Angelo Barbieri. It was Jeremy Andrews who at Barbieri's bidding got Darren a great contractor's job back at Highland and Erskerberg after Darren had been fired as a regular employee.

But Jeremy Andrews giveth and Jeremy Andrews taketh away as ordered by Barbieri, or so Darren figured. Hence Darren could well end up freed from his gold-plated bondage to Angelo Barbieri but once again fired from Highland and Erskerberg in the bargain. And there he'd be, right back where he'd been before Barbieri had saved him from drowning in debt. But by then he'd be freed of Trysta and her brood, hopefully, and as for his child support payments to Sally, well, you can't get blood from a stone and he'd be stone-broke. But free of all those familial financial drains, he could start all over again, get his real-estate management business off the ground on his own, free and clear.

Shit. How would he live in the meantime? *Where* would he live? Free of her kids, Trysta could always go back to live with her parents in Cornwells Heights and Sally, well, she'd be fine, even if he could no longer afford to pay her any child support. If Sally ever got into a bind her mother would always help her out, not to mention old money bags Silvio. But what about himself? Who could he, Darren turn to if, for all the units of real estate he bought, sold and managed for Barbieri, he found himself without a roof over his head?

"Hey, how the hell dirty is it over there?" Darren's father asked. "You keep sweeping the same spot over and over."

"Dad," Darren blurted out, "If my life all went to pot could I come and live with you?"

While Ed stood open-mouthed Donna entered the kitchen. "What, *still* cleaning up? Oh, here, I'll finish. Ed, you go relax, watch the fight with Geoffry. Darren, go help Trysta with the children."

Geoffry entered the kitchen holding up his half-drunk beer. "What's in this stuff? Tastes like pu...oh, hi, Mom. I thought you were in the living room."

"What, Geoffry, you don't like the Schöfferhafer?" asked his mother, looking slightly distressed.

"You got anything else?"

"Well, there's some Stella Artois in the basement. Darren, run down and get your brother a bottle of Stella, they're on the second shelf across from the freezer."

"They cold?" asked Geoffry.

"Well, no," said Donna, "they're on the shelf.

"Never mind, I'll drink this. How about something else for next time?"

"What kind do you prefer, dear?"

Geoffry looked at the bottle of Schöfferhofer with distain. "Anything but this crap."

Donna chuckled and shook her head. "These boys," she said to Ed.

After Ed and Darren had exited the kitchen Ed turned to his son. "Better not let your life go to pot."

Chapter Nine

Darren sat at his desk staring at his laptop screen without absorbing any of the information on the document before him. He was thinking.

His father had been right, of course. He couldn't afford to let his life go to pot. He glanced at the bottom right corner of the screen. Eight-thirty-seven a.m. He had a ten a.m. meeting at Highland and Erskerberg before which he should have a working idea – or at least a fakeable idea – of the contents of the document staring out at him from his laptop screen, something about potential accumulated cost recovery of future agglomeration economies in the Washington Square West neighborhood. But there was enough time to call Geoffry, get the ball rolling. If Darren really wanted to do this. Darren picked up his cellphone from his desk, studied it for a moment, then put it down again.

Aw, what the hell, he'd do it. It was a dangerous, crap idea, but what choice did he have?

Darren picked up his cell and dialed Geoffry's number.

"Aw, shit, man," Darren heard Geoffry's groggy voice, "the hell you calling me so early for?"

He had woken Geoffry up, the lazy slob. Excellent.

"Aw, sorry," said Darren, improvising, "I just had a breakfast meeting with Angelo."

Geoffry yawned loudly. "The fuck do I care?" He sounded irritable beyond having been woken up early. "How come *you* had breakfast with Angelo?"

"Just a little, uh, business," said Darren.

"What, to give you more money for doing squat?" Geoffry asked bitterly.

"Geoffry," Darren said, "Angelo's been underutilizing you. You remember that hundred and ten thousand we counted out last time were both in the office?"

Geoffry yawned. "Yeah?"

"Angelo gave me that money to go buy him a piece of cheap property out in Wedgefield."

"Wedgefield? The fuck does he want a piece a shit property in Wedgefield for?"

"Geoffry. Don't ask don't tell where or why Angelo Barbieri wants to stash his money." Darren lowered his voice to just above a whisper. "There's some money that it's safer to stash in a piece of shit property than in a bank. You know what I'm saying?"

"Yeah, I know about Angelo's money," Geoffry said petulantly. "I work for him too, you know."

"Which brings me to my point. So anyway, I told Angelo, just this morning, I said, 'Jesus, Angelo, between working for you and at Highland and Erskerberg, and then I got a family, I'm up to my *hole*. And now you want me to go out and find you a property in Wedgefield? I don't have *time*, Angelo,' I said. I told him, 'why don't you give Geoffry the hundred and ten and let him buy the property, and he can have the commission, 'cause, look,' I told him, 'between what you're paying me these days and what I'm bringing home from Highland and Erskerberg, I don't need the sixty thousand I'll get out of this sale.'"

"The *fuck?*" said Geoffry, now sounding wide awake, "You're getting a sixty thousand commission? For buying a piece of crap in Wedgefield?"

"Sixty or seventy. I mean, I'll find something for maybe, forty, fifty thousand, all the expenses factored in. Then I'll keep the change. It's worth it to Angelo to have somebody do this for him. You know, considering where the money's coming from. Strictly between you and me, of course."

"Hell, yeah, I'll buy him a house in fuckin' Wedgefield for seventy thousand bucks!"

Darren sighed loudly. "Well, here's the thing. I told Angelo he should let you buy the house. With me being so busy, and all." Darren sighed again. "But…"

"But what?"

"You don't want to know what Angelo said."

"Yes I want to know what he said! What'd he say?"

"No, seriously, you don't."

"Quit screwing with me, what the fuck did he say?"

Darren hesitated as if unable to bring himself to say it. "He said, 'Geoffry?'"

"That's all he said? *'Geoffry?'* What else?"

"Aw, Bro, you don't want to know."

"What else did he say!" Geoffry shouted into the phone.

Darren produced another heavy sigh. "He said, 'Geoffry?' Then he lifted one cheek off his chair and blew out this huge fart. I mean, it was massive."

"What?"

"Hey, I was offended. I wanted to say, 'WTF, man, that's my brother!' But what could I do?"

"You coulda kicked his ass, you wussy!"

"Okay, calm down, Bro. Look, you know how Angelo is. Always talking trash about everybody, it doesn't mean anything. But why I called you is, I still don't have time for this deal. You wanna do it for me? I give you the money, you go buy something, you keep the change. Angelo doesn't have to know you're doing it and not me. I can sign all the papers, he trusts me to run the whole show. Or you can sign for me, what difference does it make? Angelo will get a piggy bank property to stash his shady money in and you'll be a few shekels richer. What do you think?"

"Yeah, sure, give me the money, I can buy him a property. Wedgefield, huh? Do I actually have to go there?"

"You might. But, hey, it's fine, I mean, lots of people live there. I'll tell you what, go online, find a cheap property, call the real estate agent, tell them you want to buy the place, sight unseen, for investment purposes. Then you won't have to even go there. "

"And whatever I spend I keep the change?"

"Right. You don't have to spend much. I mean, as little as you want. Angelo doesn't care. This is just like pocket change for him, he pretty much just wants me to get rid of it for him."

"Huh, why wouldn't the son-of-a-bitch just give the money to me? I'd take it off his hands for him."

Darren laughed. "Right? But look, he practically *is* giving it to you. I mean, he's giving it to me. And I'm giving it to you. So you want to do this?"

"Yeah, okay. So what do I do again?"

"All right. You go online, type in 'Wedgefield real estate.' You see something you want to buy…"

"Something cheap, right?"

"Sure, the cheaper the better. Easier to flip down the road, right? You call the real estate agent listed, tell 'em you're paying cash and they'll take it from there. You buy it under the name of Angelo's business, SP Wrecking, right? When you found something you want to buy call me, I'll get you the cash."

"I can pay with cash?"

"Wedgefield? You want something out there, sure, you can pay in cash, those agents will take anything they can get to move one of those properties. So you'll call me when the deal is done and I'll get the cash to you. Okay?"

"Yeah."

"And remember, this is strictly between you and me. Don't mention to Angelo that you're doing the buying."

"What do you think I am, stupid?"

Darren stifled a laugh. "Okay, well, I'll let you get right on it."

"Yeah, I'll get on it," said Geoffry, yawning, "but I'm gonna go back to sleep for a while."

"Sure," Darren chuckled, "you go sleep some more. Dream of what you'll do with all the money you're gonna make."

Geoffry yawned again, a loud obnoxious yawn. "See ya."

"Yeah see ya." After he hung up Darren added, "You dumb fuck!"

"*Excuse* me?" Trysta stood in the doorway of his office holding onto Miri's car seat carrier in which the baby dozed.

"Oh, ha, ha, I was just talking to myself. About a client. It's nothing, just...nothing."

"Oh," said Trysta. She set Miri's carrier on the floor beside her.

Darren took in how gorgeous his wife looked this morning, less dragged out than she often did in the morning. Like she'd done her make-up and hair with extra care. She was wearing a clingy white pullover sweater and a pretty necklace, pretty earrings, all of it topping those sung-fitting jeans of hers. The sex had been pretty great for the last week, and even though they'd made love the night before he wouldn't mind a little roll right now, she looked so good. And after his phone call with Geoffry he was feeling like a little celebration.

"You going somewhere or something?" Darren asked her.

"I have an appointment with Dr. Cavanni."

"Dr. Cavanni? Again? Didn't you just go for a conference with her last week?"

"Yes. But I have another one."

Darren rose from his desk and approached his wife. "Another one? What, is Zach having more problems? I mean, I thought he was doing a lot better."

"He is. But Dr. Cavanni wants to see me again anyway."

"Okay." Darren wrapped his arms around Trysta's waist. "You have to go right this minute? You have time for a little...?"

"I thought you had to get to work."

"Yeah, but I could go in a little later." He nuzzled and kissed her neck. "Ummm, you smell good."

"I'm sorry, Darren, I'm kind of in a hurry right now." She pulled slightly away. "For my appointment."

"Oh, okay." Darren let her go. "Maybe later, huh?"

"Yes. Maybe later. 'Bye." Then she picked up the baby and was off.

Boy, it occurred to Darren, *when Trysta wasn't in the mood she wasn't in the mood.*

***

It was true that Trysta was in a hurry. She had just a little under an hour and a half to get Miri across town to her mother, who'd agreed to babysit for the morning, then back for her appointment with Laura. *Laura.* Trysta was already calling her Laura in her mind. Trysta tingled at the thought of Laura's touch. Trysta hoped they'd touch today. Even if it was just the touch of their hands, or maybe Laura would give her a friendly hug…oh, if that happened, Trysta would make it last forever, she'd press her breasts against Laura's, and…her daydream was cut short by the honk of an impatient car horn rudely informing her that the traffic light had changed.

***

"Where's the little princess today?" asked Dr. Cavanni after Trysta had shimmied out of her jacket and settled herself into the armchair.

"I left her with my mom."

Dr. Cavanni noted how much brighter her patient looked today than at their last session. Brighter than Dr. Cavanni had ever seen her. Glowing, in fact. Made up with care and wearing jewelry and a clingy white sweater that offered more than a hint of cleavage. Transformed. Or, as Dr. Cavanni suspected, dressed to potentially act out a budding crush on her therapist. Well, as Dr. Cavanni had learned, a passing crush, if handled carefully, could be as useful an excavation tool as any for helping a patient mine his or her psyche.

"You look nice today, Trysta," she began.

Trysta blushed with pleasure. "Thank you, Laur…Dr. Cavanni."

"It's all right. You can call me Laura if you'd like. Have you come up with any thoughts since our last session?"

"Thoughts?"

"On figuring out what you might want to do with your life?"

"Oh, well…I've been busy."

"Busy?"

"Like I always am," Trysta said, running a hand through her hair, "you know, children, baby, house, husband." *And thinking about you.*

"Anything changed since last week? Anything going on in your life that you want to talk about?" *Besides your obvious fixation with me?*

You, thought Trysta, *you're what's going on in my life.* And there were those beautiful brown eyes fixed on her again, interested in her, only her. Trysta sighed. "Well…I've been sleeping with Darren almost every night."

"Oh?"

Trysta nodded.

"Because you're still hoping to hang onto him?"

Trysta lowered her eyes. "I do need to hang onto him as long as I can." When she looked up her eyes glistened with tears. "What will I do when he leaves me?"

"Well…I believe that's what we were going to talk about. What *will* you do when Darren leaves you?"

"I don't know. I'll be…*alone.*"

"'Single,' you mean. And free to do what you want to do. Be who you want to be."

"But I don't *know* what I want to do. Or who I want to be."

"Then you just think of something to do. Think of someone you'd like to be. Then figure out a way to make it happen. Trysta, you can't depend on a husband and children to give you identity. You've been doing that your whole adult life and you yourself admit it hasn't made you especially happy."

"But with the right person I *could* be happy." Trysta sniffed and rubbed a tear from her eye. "And I could make *them* happy."

"Ummm," said Laura, perfectly aware that at the moment Trysta was more focused on playing the helpless damsel in distress – probably her tried and true method of seduction – than figuring out her life.

Dr. Cavanni was weighing whether this might be the moment to intervene and break the obvious to Trysta when Trysta stood and arched her back as if stretching so that her breasts arched forward. "Laura," she asked breathily, "does *your* husband make you happy?"

"I'm divorced," answered Dr. Cavanni.

"You're divorced?" Trysta's eyes lit up.

"Yes, I am. Ten years now."

"Do you have…a boyfriend?

Laura shook her head. "No."

"Oh," said Trysta, smiling brightly.

"However I'm not lonely. And I'm not looking for a partner or a lover or a friend." Laura smiled warmly. "Okay?"

Trysta looked momentarily deflated. Then she smiled nonchalantly and shrugged. "Okay." She sat back down.

"That being said, is there anything else you'd like to ask me?"

"Oh," said Trysta. "Well…Why did *you* get divorced?"

"Because my husband was sleeping with the nanny."

"The *nanny*? Huh, what a jerk!"

"I should clarify that my husband sleeping with the nanny was just the immediate cause. I suppose the long-term underlying cause was that I wanted to sleep with the nanny, too."

"What?"

Laura laughed. "I'm gay."

"What? Gay?"

Laura nodded.

"Gay? You mean, like…*lesbian?"*

"Yes. Lesbian."

"But…you don't *look* lesbian."

Laura laughed again.

"I mean, you don't have that haircut or, you know, the clothes."

Laura shrugged. "Don't need the haircut or the clothes to be a lesbian."

"But…are you sure? I mean, that you're *really* gay? And not, like, maybe you just fell in love with that one nanny that one time?"

"I didn't fall in love with the nanny. My husband did. I just wanted to have sex with her. But I didn't have sex with her. Not the least reason being that she didn't want to have sex with me. But back to your question. I've never been sexually attracted to men."

"But…why did you marry one, then?"

Laura sighed. "You have to remember, when I was young being gay was not nearly as socially acceptable as it is now, not that it is everywhere even now, and the subject was definitely not as open or as talked about. I played girls' sports, there was always a lot of excitement, adrenalin, camaraderie, hugging, closeness. I loved my girls and they loved me. We even joked about having 'girl crushes.' But if there was anything more going on among any of us it was well repressed. Or, being teen-aged girls, as yet undeveloped. Remember, girls develop sexually, I mean up here," Laura pointed to her head, "later than boys do."

"Wow," said Trysta, in a state of wonderment at this new information, "That is so, so…"

Dr. Cavanni waited for Trysta to find the word, but when it became clear that her patient was for the moment wordless, she continued. "Anyway, it never occurred to me that I felt any differently than all the other girls I knew. As far as getting married…I was in love, or thought I was. But look, love isn't always tied to sexual attraction, is it? It can be tied to social norms. I was taught that girls dated and fell in love with boys. All my friends dated and fell in love with boys. So I dated and fell in love with boys. And then I married one, just like all the other girls did. And love…what is love, or the illusion of love, really? One can be in love with a person's looks, status, ideals, lifestyle, whatever. One can be as in love with the whole benefits package a person can offer as a mate as with the person them self. Or one can be *more* in love with that benefits package than the person them self. Does that make any sense?"

"Yeah," said Trysta, still speechless, "yeah."

"So I got married, eventually figured it out, then got divorced."

"But what did your parents say?"

Laura shrugged. "Fortunately for me, my parents run with a pretty liberal group. And besides, they never much liked the man I married. Or his family."

"My father didn't like Silvio because he thought Silvio got me pregnant when I was eighteen. But he still had a fit when I left Silvio. I don't even know if he'll let me move back home with Miri if Darren leaves me. Did you get to keep your house?"

"No. I moved into a small apartment for a while until the divorce proceedings were finished and the assets divied. Then I found a new place."

"Was it hard for you? Being a single mother?"

"My ex-husband got full custody of our children."

"What? You mean they took your children away from you because you were gay?"

"Not at all. We agreed it would be best for the children. After all, he had the nanny."

"You just…agreed to give up your children?"

"I didn't give them up. I saw them often. I still do."

"But…didn't people think you were a horrible mother?"

Laura shrugged again. "I did what I thought was best for my children and myself. And there was no big ugly custody battle. What's horrible about that?"

Again Trysta was left speechless at the strange new concept that a woman could give up her children and not be a horrible mother.

"And what if some people did say behind my back that I was a horrible mother? What did I care? I knew I wasn't a *horrible* mother." Laura paused and said with a mischievous twinkle in her eye, "Maybe just a *terrible* mother." Her tone turned serious again. "But those people who said I was, they weren't paying my bills. They weren't supporting my children. I was paying my own bills. I was paying child support. You see, Trysta, when you're living your own life, paying your own bills, it doesn't matter what people say about you."

"It doesn't?"

"Why would it?"

"But…giving up your children…and being *gay*…"

"To thine ownself be true, Trysta. You should try it. It will change your world."

Later that night after pretending to make passionate love to Darren while fantasizing about Laura, Trysta stood in the shower and let the water wash over her. *Could I be gay?* She lifted a strand of her long hair, long her whole life, and imagined cropping it short. *Would Laura like that?* She pictured herself dressed in baggy pants and mannish shirts instead of the tight fitting, sexy clothes that had always felt like a required dress code. She imagined living and sleeping with another woman. *Gay. Gay. Gay.* She repeated the word over and over in her mind, trying it on. The thought was frightening. And exhilarating.

She recalled Ms. Thomas, Elizabeth Thomas, her math teacher during her senior year of high school. Alezziebeth Thomas, some of the kids called her, Lezzie the Lesbian, but that was only because of the man-tailored pants and shirts she wore, and her reddish-blond hair, clipped short in the back but long on top. Slim like Laura, but younger and shorter and not as friendly and cheerful. She was strict and took no excuses and some of the kids called her a lesbian bitch. But she'd always been nice to Trysta. Maybe "nice" wasn't the word…more like, "approving," which actually meant more to Trysta than nice. Lots of people were nice to her. Especially the boys. But Ms. Thomas would look at Trysta's homework or a test she was handing back and nod and say softly, "Good job, Trysta," or "Very nice work," which would make Trysta's heart flutter. Once she told Trysta that she had a lot of ability. Once she held up a test paper of Trysta's and said, "Is Trysta Wells the only one in this class who knows what to do with a parabola?" Trysta's heart had fluttered but then the class snickered and after that *Trysta knows what to do with a parabola* became kind of a thing around school for a while.

But Trysta just giggled it away except for the time when her boyfriend Jeremy DeCiccio said it then pulled out his penis and stuck it into her hand, then her mouth, then anywhere else he felt like sticking it, and she would have hated him if she hadn't been so in love with him and had already missed a period.

I'm gay, she thought. And – dared she think it? – *I'm a horrible mother.* Well, no, not *horrible,* maybe…just…*terrible. I'm gay and I'm a terrible mother like Laura and I'm going to make enough money to not care who says so and I want Silvio to take all my children, even Miri, so that I can finally have my own life and be…gay. But I'm not going to let Silvio know that's what I want. I'll make him keep fighting and spending money on his lawyer. I'm not going to let anybody know what I really am and I what I want. Except Laura.*

Trysta yelped and jumped away from the stream of water, which had gone cold.

Chapter Ten

Trysta was waiting by the front door with Silvia Miri in her arms when Silvio arrived to pick up the kids. As soon as she saw his red plumber's van pull into the driveway she strode out of the house to the van.

"I know you don't want to see your daughter, but maybe she wants to see you," Trysta snipped.

Silvio rolled his eyes in exasperation "Geeze, Trysta, would you stop it? You know she's not my daughter. Now where are my kids?"

"Silvia is your children's sister. *Our* children's sister. They love her. And she loves them. And now," Trysta's eyes filled with tears, "you want to tear these children apart from each other!" A loud sob escaped from her throat.

"Fine!" Silvio shouted without meaning to, "You want me to take this little girl off your hands so you can go sleeping around with every man you meet? Fine, give her to me! I'll take her and I'll raise her along with all the others! Give her to me right now!"

"Oh, how *could* you?" Trysta sobbed. "Screaming right at poor, innocent little Silvia and making her cry, how *could* you!" Trysta held the wailing baby close. "Hush, my precious," she cooed as she hurried away from Silvio's van, stopping on the porch and using her sleeve to wipe away her tears, which had ceased flowing as soon as she turned away from Silvio.

Silvio sat shaking his head, his fingers pressed against his eyes. "What's the matter with me?" he mumbled, "What's the *matter* with me, what's the *matter* with me?"

"Daddy!" Silvio looked up to see his children approaching his van, Sam waving excitedly. He got out to help them load their back packs and duffle bags into the van.

"Daddy," Sam cried breathlessly, "Mommy says to tell you"

"Shut up, Sam," said Zach.

"Hey, you don't talk to your little sister like that, okay?" said Silvio.

"Yeah, you don't talk to me like that, Zach," huffed Sam.

"And not me, either," huffed Trina.

"What?" said Zach with mock indignity, "I didn't tell *you* to shut up."

"Zach," said Silvio sternly.

"Ooookay," sighed Zach.

Ten minutes later when they were headed east on the Schuylkill Expressway, away from the upscale western suburb of New Conshohocken towards the working-class eastern suburb of Cornwells Heights, Silvio cleared his throat and said, "So Sam. What did Mom say to tell me?"

"Don't worry about it, Dad," said Zach.

"Daddy asked *me*," said Sam.

"Mommy said," Trina piped up, "to tell you"

"*Triiiiinnnnnaaaaa!*"

Silvio braked and pulled over to the shoulder. "Hey, Sam! No screaming like that. Not in this van, you hear?"

"But *I* want to tell you what Mommy said!" Sam wailed.

"Okay," said Silvio. "Tell me."

Sam shot her siblings and imperious look. "Mommy said to tell you that she hopes you're happy. Are you happy, Daddy?"

Silvio pulled back out onto the highway. "Yeah," he murmured, "yeah."

***

Charleston Tilley was curious as to why Silvio had shown up at his office without Sally. Of course the last time the couple came to seek counsel about the child who was causing so much tumult in their lives there had been an unpleasantly emotional scene, so perhaps Silvio had been wise to come alone this time and to handle the issue by himself. Charleston only hoped that Silvio and Sally had thoroughly discussed the matter and were in agreement. But of course it was none of his business.

Charleston listened while the young plumber described the latest twist in the recently complicated saga of his life. Then Charleston turned off the Dictaphone on his desk and said, "So, the circumstances being that Silvia appears to be biologically neither your child nor Darren's, and Darren having made it clear that he has no interest in raising her..."

"Yeah, he made that pretty clear when he called to tell me she was mine. I mean, he thought she was mine. Because she's not his. But I know she's not mine. You know, 'cause of the alleles, and all."

Charleston nodded. "Have you told Darren that?"

"No. I never called him back."

"And I don't recommend that you do. At this time I'd keep all communication with Darren and Trysta to the necessary minimum."

"It's not like I'm not trying. But whenever I go to pick up my kids all Trysta wants to do is play games with me and mess with my head."

Charleston sighed. "Unfortunately you can't control your ex-wife's behavior."

"Yeah, well, these days I'm having a hard time controlling my own. Which is not helping things."

Charleston nodded again. "But what you've decided, then, is that you'd like to have some sort of custodial relationship with Silvia if it were possible. Even though she's not your biological child."

"She may not be mine but she's the sister of my children. They should be together."

"Unfortunately, the way the law in written, you have no legal claim on Silvia, even if you gain custody of her siblings. She is legally Trysta's and Darren's child even if Darren is not the biological father. Now, the biological father could, theoretically, show up and sue for custody of his child..."

"Ha, that's not gonna happen," Silvio chuckled bitterly.

"No, it doesn't appear likely. Though, trust me, stranger things have happened. But let's assume that it won't. You, however have no claim on Silvia. Now, there is such a thing as non-parental custody, which might be granted to a non-biological parent only under the most extreme circumstances, which Silvia's does not appear to be."

"Yeah, well, I don't know what goes on in that house," said Silvio.

"Trust me, convoluted and unusual as this whole situation is, so far I've heard nothing that would warrant a court taking Silvia from her mother. Courts take the rights of biological parents very seriously."

"Yeah, okay."

"But there is also such a thing as non-parental *guardianship*. It's called consent guardianship because the parents give their written consent for a non-parent to have custody of their child. Consent guardianship is the quickest and easiest way for a person to obtain custody of a child that isn't theirs. However," Charleston raised a finger for emphasis, "the biological parents keep the right to revoke consent and take custody back. And again, both parents must agree to hand the child over to the custody of the non-parent. And the non-biological parent who's been given custody of the child can likewise end the agreement at anytime. Does that make sense, Mr. Jablonski?"

"Yeah," said Silvio. "I mean, it doesn't, but it does."

"So then, I believe that in your case custodial guardianship would be about the only option. Now, from what you've told me, it seems rather doubtful that your ex-wife would be willing to sign over full-time guardianship of Silvia to you, even if her husband, who is also the baby's legal parent, would."

"Oh yeah, I'm sure Darren would," said Silvio. "But Trysta? No, she wouldn't just give me Silvia with no strings attached."

"Your custody hearing is in two weeks, correct?"

"Yeah, that's right."

"Assuming you were to win physical and legal custody of your children – either partial, which is all but guaranteed, or full, which is not – might it be within the realm of possibility that Trysta would be willing to grant you part-time custodial guardianship of Silvia? Or name you as her daughter's legal guardian in addition to herself and her husband? After all, as you pointed out, Silvia is the other children's sister and chances are Trysta may eventually come around to see that it would be beneficial for Silvia to be with her siblings when they are with you – if not all of the time at least some of the time – and for you to be in a position to be able take care of her as a legal guardian."

"Like I said, I can't see Trysta giving me anything if there's nothing in it for her."

"She may change her mind over time, and if and when she does we can re-visit the possibility of pursuing a custodial guardianship. So don't give up hope. But in the meantime we need to get through the hearing and the judge's decision." Charleston looked over some paperwork on his desk. "Now, as far as I can see, your ex-wife does not yet appear to have procured any legal representation for the upcoming hearing. Which is strange."

"It's probably because Darren won't pay for a lawyer. He wants me to get my kids back. He doesn't want to have to raise them. I think Trysta really thought she could convince me to take her back. I think her plan was to leave Darren and come back to me with the kids. See, I've got some money now. But I don't want her back. I just want my kids. She's using the baby as bait."

"Silvio?"

"Yeah?"

"Whatever you do, don't bite."

***

Sally picked up her cell phone from her desk, smiling when she saw Silvio's name on the screen. Silvio often called her once or twice during the day, or she called him, just for a quick chat that always ended with "Love you." But for the past week he hadn't called her. All the calls between them had come from her. Well, maybe he was having a busy week. He probably was, since he hadn't been over to her house much, either. But whenever they were together he seemed fine, no longer obsessed with Trysta and her baby. So that was good. And now he was calling her again, so that was good, too.

"Hey, Babe," she said. But her smile faded as she listened. "So you went to see Mr. Tilley?" *Without me?* She thought. She continued to listen. "Yeah, of course I'm okay with it, I mean, I told you I would be, but…" *But why didn't you tell me you'd changed your mind about Silvia? Why didn't you tell me you were going to see Charleston Tilley? Why didn't you ask me to come with you?* "Oh. Yeah. Okay. No, it's fine." *It's not fine.* "It's good." *It's not good.* "Yeah, I'm good." *No, I'm not good.* "Okay, see you later. Yeah, 'bye. Love you, t…" Sally moved the phone from her ear and stared at the screen. Silvio had already hung up.

"Bad news?"

Sally looked up from her phone to see Joanne standing next to her desk. "Well, no…I mean, not exactly, I guess. I mean…I don't know. That was Silvio."

Joanne sighed. "Oh, boy." She glanced at her watch. "It's caffeine-thirty. Finish up what you're doing and meet me in the break room in fifteen minutes."

Sally and Joanne sipped their mediocre break-room lattes.

"It's not so much that he's decided that he wants to try and get custody of Silvia – or guardianship, he called it, which sounds more like kid-sharing – it's that he didn't tell me. And he went and saw Charleston without even telling me he was going to. And then just now when he called to tell me what he did he told me so fast and then hung up, like he didn't even want to talk about it with me."

"Bingo," said Joanne.

"What?"

"He didn't want to talk about it with you."

"But…why wouldn't he want to talk about it with me?" Sally began tearing up.

"Well," said Joanne, "what happened last time you talked about it?"

"Last time?" Sally sighed. "We both ended up getting upset with each other."

"And the time before that?" asked Joanne.

Sally thought for a moment. "We kind of had a fight."

"And the time before that?"

"Look," said Sally, "it's just that this is all we talk about anymore and every time we talk about it we just go round and round because Silvio can't make up his mind."

"So maybe talking about it wasn't helping him make up his mind. Maybe it was something he needed to figure out by himself. Maybe he needed a little quiet, a little, you know, reflection."

"Okay, I guess I get that. But then going to see Charleston without me?"

"What happened last time you went to see Charleston together?" Joanne asked.

Sally sighed. "We ended up arguing and crying in front of him."

"I rest my case," said Joanne.

"But…people who are in love are supposed to be able to do the important things together." Sally wiped away the tear that began trickling down her cheek.

Joanne patted Sally's hand. "Baby, people who are in love can't always do the important things together. Sometimes the only way a problem can be solved is to divide and conquer. Sometimes he's gonna have his problems and sometimes you're gonna have yours, and if you're still on board with him helping you raise Josh and maybe David and you helping him raise his kids, including this newest addition, if she does become an addition…are you still on board with all that?"

"Of course," said Sally. "I'm still one hundred percent on board."

"Then you gotta sit tight on this one and let Silvio figure it out. And give it time, okay?"

"Okay," Sally sighed.

Joanne checked her watch. "And speaking of time, it's time to put these sorry excuses of a latte out of their misery and get back to work."

***

After his meeting with Charleston Silvio had called Sally right away, while he was still parked at the downtown garage near Charleston's office. Now as he headed down I-95 towards Northeast Philadelphia and back to Quick and Reliable he wondered if Sally was mad at him. He didn't feel good about that phone call. He didn't feel good about going to see Charleston without her. He didn't even feel good coming to a decision about Silvia without letting Sally know. But the thought of hashing it out again with Sally, of doubling the input, doubling the questions, doubling the concerns, doubling the emotion was more than his brain could handle. He already felt like his brain was full to bursting with his own thoughts and worries. There was hardly room in his head for anything else right now and he had to force himself to focus on work, at least for the rest of the day.

If only he could just dump out everything that was weighing on his mind and heart, tell someone what was going on in his life, give someone a blow-by-blow including what he was thinking, what he was feeling, how confused and even afraid he was at this minute. He wished someone were holding him close right now, stroking his head and listening and telling him that everything would be okay.

He wished that someone were Sally.

He pulled into the parking lot behind his office, pulled out his cell phone and pulled up Sally's number. She was probably busy at work. He had to get back to work. She was probably mad at him. He was afraid to call her. He slipped his phone back into his pocket.

Chapter Eleven

"The hell is this?" Darren muttered, turning over the statement that he held in his hand. He'd almost thrown out the envelope it had arrived in, figuring it to be among the daily junk that was usually deposited in his mailbox.

Darren stepped out of his office into the hallway to see Trysta bundling Miri into her car seat. "Hey, what's this bill from Dr. Cavanni for a thirty dollar co-pay? How come she sent it to me? She's seeing Zach, right? How come it says treatment for you?"

"What?" Trysta took the bill from Darren and looked it over. She wanted to kick herself – had it really not occurred to her that of course Laura's bill would be sent to Darren?

"How the hell did they screw this up?" said Darren. "Well, screw it, I'll send it to Silvio and tell him he's gotta deal with it. Like I don't already have enough to do."

"Why don't you just pay it," said Trysta, "it's only thirty dollars." *I'll have to get Laura to give me the bills from now on,* she thought.

"Pay it? Are you kidding? *Of course* I'm not gonna pay it!"

"I just meant," she moved so close to Darren that he could smell the clean scent of her hair, "why bother yourself over such a little thing?" She put her arms around his waist, not sure what her next move should be. She had to get out of here to get Miri over to her mother's or she'd be late for Laura.

Darren nuzzled her neck. "Don't worry about it, Babe." Miri began whimpering in her carrier. Darren looked over at the baby then noticed his wife was wearing a jacket. "Hey, where you going with Miri, anyway?"

"I'm just going to drop her off at my mom's." Trysta had a sudden sinking feeling that this wasn't going to work.

"Why? You gotta go somewhere?"

I'm too tired for this, she thought, pulling away from Darren and picking up Miri's carrier.

"I have to see Dr. Cavanni," she said tersely, "and if I don't leave now I'll be late." She turned from Darren and headed for the back door that led out to the garage.

Darren hurried after his wife, beating her to the door. "Wait...you're seeing Zach's psychologist again? Is that what this bill is about? You go to talk about Zach and *I* gotta pay?"

Trysta pulled in a deep breath. "Dr. Cavanni is my therapist, too. I've been seeing her for *me*."

"For *you*? What? And you don't even tell me? I gotta find out when I get the bill?"

"It's only thirty dollars!" Trysta pushed the bill at Darren and pulled open the door then hurried with Miri to her midnight blue SUV.

Darren dropped the bill and hurried behind his wife and, out of habit, opened the door for her and helped her get the carrier strapped in. "How come *you're* seeing the psychologist? Trysta, what's going on? What's the matter?"

Trysta slid into the front seat of the car. "What's the matter? You want to know *what's the matter*?" She slammed the door and started the engine then pulled out of the garage and down the driveway.

Darren, drop-jawed, watched his wife's car take off down the street. Then he headed back inside, muttering, "I'm the one who needs a goddamn psychologist."

***

That actually wasn't too bad, thought Trysta as she headed east on Conshohocken Road towards the Schuylkill Expressway. She couldn't believe she hadn't thought about that thirty-dollar co-pay bill going to Darren. But it was probably just as well that the bill arrived as she was rushing out the door. Now she'd have time to think up something to tell Darren, something to make it sound like it was perfectly normal that she should be seeing Laura. And if Darren flipped out or got nasty about it she could blame him for being so, so…well, she'd think of something to blame him for, God knows there was plenty. Or she could tell him that she was just trying to learn to be a better mother to her children and a better wife to him. The tears welled up in her eyes as in the eyes of a well-conditioned actress as she rehearsed the scene in her mind. Not that she wanted to share Laura with Darren, but what could she do? Darned bill.

After she dropped Miri off at her mother's house Trysta was bathed in the happy glow of anticipation of her appointment with Laura. It was worth a drive across the city and back again just to have this alone time with Laura, freed from the demands of motherhood for one hour, to have Laura see her as a woman, an attractive, desirable woman, and not as a bedraggled housewife and mother.

Maybe she should start by telling Laura about her terrible fight with Darren this morning – well, it hadn't been all that terrible – she'd rushed out before it could go anywhere – but Darren did yell at her, and if she burst into Laura's office all upset, her eyes reddened with tears – thank goodness she always used a dependable brand of waterproof mascara – maybe Laura would wrap her arms around Trysta to comfort her. And while still in her arms Trysta could reveal, voice trembling, that she was gay. She'd then look into Laura's eyes and smile through her tears, and who knew where it all might lead?

**

"Trysta, are you all right?" asked Laura Cavanni, deftly stepping aside as Trysta rushed towards her, then taking her by the arm and leading her to the chair across from her desk. "What's wrong?"

Trysta felt a sting of disappointment at having missed Laura's arms, but she obediently sat down. "Well," she sniffled, "Darren and I got into a huge fight this morning and he yelled at me like he always does."

"I see," said Dr. Cavanni. "Did he physically harm or abuse you in any way?"

"No, I guess not," Trysta said, wiping her eyes.

"Did he grab you or push you or touch you in a way that made you uncomfortable or frightened?"

"No," said Trysta.

"You're all right, then?" said Dr. Cavanni.

"I guess," Trysta sighed. It was clear to Trysta that the original scenario she'd planned for today wasn't going to play out as she'd imagined. She might as well let the thing with Darren go.

"He was just…being Darren, I guess."

"What do you mean?"

"Oh, he over-reacts sometimes."

He *over-reacts?* Thought Laura, but to Trysta she said, "And what was he over-reacting about?"

"Oh, nothing." And yet there was something about Laura Cavanni, standing by her desk, listening as if she were hanging on Trysta's every word, looking intently at Trysta as if she were gazing into her soul with those deep, calm, lovely almond eyes, that compelled Trysta to tell her the truth. After all, wasn't Laura the one and only person Trysta *could* be completely truthful with? Wasn't that why Trysta loved her? Trysta sighed. "Actually, he was angry about your bill. The thirty-dollar co-pay. It arrived in the mail today."

"He was angry about my bill? He didn't want to pay for your treatment?"

"Not exactly. See, he thought it was a bill sent to him by mistake for one of Zach's appointments. And then I, uh, told him to just pay it. And that's when he, uh, got a little mad at me. So then I told him the bill wasn't for Zach. That I was seeing you, too."

"He didn't know you were seeing me?"

"No," Trysta said sheepishly. "I didn't tell him."

"And he just found out this morning when he got the bill."

Trysta nodded.

"So you told him you were seeing me. And then what happened?"

Trysta shrugged. "Well, nothing. I jumped in the car and left with Miri. I didn't want to be late for my appointment. He just kind of stood at the door looking surprised."

"Are you afraid to return home to him? Afraid he might harm or intimidate you in some way?"

Trysta giggled. "Darren? No. He just makes a lot of noise sometimes. I guess Darren's not all that bad. As men go. But I don't love him. I've never loved him. I couldn't love him." Trysta knew that this was her moment. She stood and approached Laura, the tears once again welling up in her eyes. "I could never really love any of those men, because..." In a quick movie she wrapped her arms around Laura so that their bodies were pressed so close that Laura felt a tear drop onto her neck. "I'm *gay*! And *you're* the one that I"

"Trysta, stop," Dr. Cavanni cut her off. She gently released herself from Trysta's embrace and stepped back. "This can't be."

Trysta looked stricken. "But it's true," she cried, "I *am* gay! And I *do* lo"

"Stop," Laura cut her off again. "Yes, I believe you. And let me be the first to welcome you out. You know, I thought perhaps my sharing my own story might help you to this realization about yourself and I'm glad it did. But"

"What? You *knew* I was gay? Before I even did? How?"

"Didn't know. Just suspected." Dr. Cavanni smiled. "I've read a book or two on the subject."

Trysta smiled through her tears. "You see?" she said breathlessly, "You know me better than anyone. You know me better than I know myself." Again she threw her arms around Laura. "How could I *not* lo"

"*Trysta.*" Dr. Cavanni again pulled away, but this time she held Trysta's hands in hers, mostly to keep her patient from throwing herself at her again. "All of what you say may be true. But as I started to tell you, we cannot under any circumstances pursue a relationship other than that of doctor and patient."

"But why?"

Laura let go of Trysta's hands and stepped back. "First of all, I could lose my license for getting involved with a patient."

"But I wouldn't tell anyone," Trysta cried.

"In the wise words of Emily Dickinson, 'You cannot fold a flood and put it in your drawer, because the winds would find it out and tell your cedar floor.' "

"What?"

Dr. Cavanni looked Trysta directly in the eye. "You know what I'm saying. Right?"

"But if we really loved each other…"

"Oh, that would be a disaster," said Dr. Cavanni. "But trust me, Trysta, we don't."

"But I do!" Trysta sobbed, "I do love you!"

"All right, I won't dispute you. Maybe you do for now. You won't be the first patient who's fallen in love with her therapist."

Trysta stepped close to Laura. "Is that all I am to you? A patient?"

She tried to put her hand on Laura's cheek but Laura intercepted her and pushed her away.

"You're my patient, I'm your therapist, that's it," Laura said in the I-mean-business voice she learned how to use during her high school and college team-captain days. "But that's over right now if you continue to pursue me. Got it, Trysta?"

Trysta stood for a moment drop-jawed, her cheeks red with anger and humiliation. "I don't need to pursue anybody!" she cried before storming out of Dr. Cavanni's office.

Laura shook her head. Yeah, right, you don't. She hurried to her office door and stepped into her waiting room just as Trysta was exiting. Trysta slammed the door behind her. Laura opened the waiting room door and stood in the doorway. She called to Trysta's back as Trysta hurried down the hallway. "You know, Trysta, I'm far more valuable to you as a therapist than as a lover."

Trysta stopped.

Dr. Cavanni continued talking. "There's a world of potential lovers and lots of love to go around out there. But a good therapist is hard to find. Think about it."

Trysta turned around but Laura Cavanni was already gone.

Slowly, Trysta headed back to her therapist's office. She knocked on the closed door. Laura opened the door and Trysta entered then sat meekly in the chair, looking at her hands.

Dr. Cavanni handed Trysta a box of Kleenex. "Here. Now dry your eyes and tell me anything you've ever been good at."

***

So now *Trysta* was seeing the psychologist? The hell was that all about? Trysta had always hated that Zach was seeing Dr. Cavanni, fought it tooth and nail. Now *she* was seeing Dr. Cavanni? And why hadn't she told him about it? Well, it's not like they communicated much anyway these days. Except for the sex. The sex had been pretty good lately. Maybe the psychologist had something to do with that. Still, Darren could hardly wrap his head around the thought of Trysta opening her soul to Dr. Cavanni, who she couldn't stand. In fact he couldn't picture Trysta opening her soul to anybody.

Well, he didn't have time today – or room in his throbbing, overwrought brain – to ruminate over what Trysta was up to at the moment or why.

The godawful rush-hour traffic into downtown Philly had thankfully thinned out, as it typically had on mornings when Darren went in a little later to Highland and Erskerberg, as he did on most mornings. Except on mornings when there was a meeting, he could basically go in at whatever time he wanted. Or work from home. So long as he got the job done. Which he always did. God knows how, the chaotic, uber-stressful six-ring circus his home life was. And then the nightmare of being under Angelo Barbieri's thumb, lucrative nightmare though it was. Well, that nightmare would hopefully soon be over if his plan went accordingly. Chances were more than even that he'd lose his job at Highland and Erskerberg in the bargain. If being fired from two jobs was the worst that happened today he'd consider himself lucky. If Barbieri decided to exact his revenge in a worse way, that would be not so lucky. But this was the long shot he had to go for, and today was the day it would play out. Trysta better enjoy her psychologist appointments while Darren still had health insurance.

***

"Well," said Trysta, wiping her eyes, "I was pretty good at math."

"Math? Interesting," said Dr. Cavanni. She jotted a few words down in a notebook she'd grabbed from her desk.

"In high school, I mean. See, there was this teacher in my senior year – Ms. Thomas – and she always praised my work in front of the class, she said I was the only one who knew what to do with a parabola – well, I *was* the only one, somehow it came easy to me – but then, well, she was a lesbian, so…"

"So what? And *why* do you say she was a lesbian?"

Trysta shrugged. "Everybody said she was. Because of how she dressed and wore her hair."

Dr Cavanni laughed. "Of course how one dresses and wears one's hair determines whether one is a lesbian."

Trysta blushed. "Well, she was strict, too."

"Good for her," Dr. Cavanni said. "But you say she was nice to you?"

Trysta thought for a moment. "Not really nice, I guess. She just made me feel smart. Smarter than anyone else did."

"I expect it's because you *were* smart. Smarter than you let anyone else know."

Trysta blushed again.

"But all right, so we know you're good in math. How are you with computers?"

"I worked with a computer at Highland and Erskerberg. Even though I was just a receptionist I had to do all kinds of data entry. I was pretty good at figuring things out on my own."

"Okay, well, that's a good start. But before we talk about where your life might go from here, I'd like to give you some advice. Not as your therapist but as woman who's a little older than you and who's been around the block a time or two. Okay?"

"Okay."

"First all, stop chaining your destiny to a man – or, in the future, a woman – who you think is going to be your salvation or hand you on a platter the life you think you want. From now on, you shape your own life, good or bad. You may not have a clue how to do that at the moment, but your mission is to figure it out. Understand?

Trysta nodded, head lowered.

"And flirting, manipulating, playing games, playing the damsel in distress, disseminating drama, those are not good strategies, they haven't worked all that well for you and so you don't need to use them anymore, got it?"

Trysta nodded again, her eyes filling with tears. A moment later she was sobbing loudly into her hands.

Dr. Cavanni sighed. "And Trysta, the crying? That's gotta go." Again she handed the box of Kleenex on her desk to Trysta.

"But you're *yelling* at me," Trysta cried as she reached for the Kleenex.

"Oh, come on, I'm *not* yelling at you…okay, I am. All right, there's something for us to work on right there. From now on when somebody yells at you, don't cry."

"Okay," Trysta sniffled meekly, looking and sounding every bit the damsel in distress.

"Aw, don't you get it, Trysta? *Women can't cry.* Not if we want to accomplish anything. Oh, maybe crying will get you little worthless trinkets from time to time. But if you want to really make it in the world you've got to turn off the waterworks. Trust me."'

"Oh." Trysta immediately blotted away the last tear, wiped her nose and the tossed the damp Kleenex into the trash can next to her chair. "So…what, you're telling me that if I want to make it I can never cry again?"

Dr. Cavanni gazed at her patient for a moment in wonder. *Frankly, my dear you've missed your calling to the stage,* she wanted to say, but instead said, "No, of course I don't mean you can *never* cry again. I mean don't cry just because somebody's yelling at you. Or because your feelings have been dinged. Or as a defense mechanism. Or an offense mechanism. You've just got to drop crying as part of your strategy. Formulate a new strategy. Look, you're so conditioned to behave as you do. We're all conditioned to behave as we do. It's going to take some conscious practice to change the problematic feelings and responses that are keeping you tied to unproductive relationships and outcomes in your life. Do you get what I'm saying?"

"Yeah," Trysta sighed. She hunched over, propped her elbows against her knees, pressed her fingertips against her eyes then rested her chin in her hands. "I just don't know how I'm supposed to do that. I'm about to lose my children, lose my husband, lose my security, lose myself... "

"*Find* your security. *Find* yourself. Your best, healthiest, happiest self living the best, healthiest, happiest life that you can no matter what obstacles lie in your way."

Trysta looked up at Dr. Cavanni, her eyes starting to fill again. "How?"

"Pinch yourself. Look up. Think of something funny."

"*What?*"

"You're about to start to cry. Pinch yourself. Roll your eyes. Quick."

Trysta did as she was told. "Wow, that works."

"As for getting your act together, that's what your therapy is for. I'm here to help you slash your way through the thorny jungle of issues that are entrapping not only you but others whose lives are intertwined with yours."

"Wow," Trysta repeated, "That is so..."

"Right," Dr. Cavanni cut her off in mid-thought. "The upshot being that I believe it would be beneficial for you to be in therapy for a while, either with me or someone else."

Trysta eyes widened in dismay. "Someone else? No, no, I want to stay with you."

"In which case, as I've been *trying* to tell you, you're going to have to figure out a plan for your future. And your future therapy. I doubt Darren's going to continue covering your co-pay when you're not married anymore."

Trysta looked crushed. Dr. Cavanni added, "But we've already figured out that you're good at math. There are a number of paths you could take to monetize that ability, especially if you had some computer chops to go with it. You say you did some data entry at your job. Any other computer experience at all? In high school, maybe?"

Trysta looked down at her hands. She wondered if she should tell Laura, if she even *wanted* to tell her, about the Info Tech class.

It hadn't even been Trysta's class, it had been Jeremy DeCiccio's class, an elective he'd taken senior year of high school because he thought it sounded cool. If there was one thing Jeremy was totally about, it was cool. But the class had been full not of cool, popular jock-types like himself, but of the school's few brainy math and computer-nerd-types who were too consumed with writing programs and designing websites and getting into Penn or Drexel or MIT to care about the presence of Jeremy DeCiccio among them, and he couldn't get even the ugliest girls in the class to do his homework for him or slip him the test answers.

One night when Jeremy and Trysta were up in Jeremy's room doing homework, supposedly, except that Jeremy barely kept his big hands off her for five minutes, Jeremy began cursing at his laptop and complaining that he was going to flunk this fucking Info Tech course if he couldn't get some geek to do the homework for him. He struggled with the assignment for a few minutes more then said, "Fuck it," swiveled his desk chair around and pulled Trysta, who was lying on the bed next to his desk working on her math, onto his lap.

While he kissed and pawed her Trysta looked over his shoulder at the lines of computer language on his laptop screen. "This looks kind of like a binary equation," she said.

Jeremy stopped unbuttoning her blouse and swiveled the chair back around to look at the screen. "Can you figure that out?" he asked her, rotating her on his lap so that she faced forward, her back to his face.

"I don't know, maybe," she said. "Let me look at it. Are there any instructions, or any sample problems, or anything?"

Jeremy pulled up the lesson for Trysta to read. "Here, knock yourself out, Baby." He wrapped his arms around her from behind and continued fiddling with her blouse buttons.

Trysta tried to slap away his hands. "I can't concentrate with you doing that," she said.

"Yeah, well, *I* can't concentrate with *you* doing *that*," he said, and moved her hand over his erection. He moved her back to the bed and kissed her. "Take off your clothes and blow me first," he said softly. "Then you can help me with that computer stuff."

And so it became their ritual that, besides doing his math homework for him, Trysta would tackle his I.T. homework as well, fiddling around with codes and web designs and figuring out on her own enough about the basics of programming to do a passable job on the take-home projects that were graded as tests. And while Tryst worked at his laptop Jeremy liked to have her sit on his lap facing forward so that he could feel her up while she worked and coo into her ear what he wanted to do to her, more often than not eventually doing it.

"So yes, I know a little about computers," Trysta added bitterly after she'd told Laura about Jeremy's Info Tech class.

"Hmmm. Sounds as if you have a natural affinity for I.T. That's good. Computer coding is a hot career field right now."

"Oh, no," said Trysta, unconsciously crossing her arms. "After what Jeremy did to me, I'd *never* want to work with computers."

"What, never?"

"No, never."

What, *never?* Laura wanted to come back, but of course the old Gilbert and Sullivan joke would have been highly inappropriate and unprofessional and the reference would doubtless have been lost on Trysta anyway. Instead she said with a shrug, "Well, women have had to do worse things for money. And I.T. work pays pretty well, from what I hear."

Trysta suddenly perked up. "It does?"

"From what I hear."

"How much?"

"I can't give you a figure, but I'd say considerably more than receptionist or waitress work."

Trysta pondered for a moment. "I'd have to go back to school, though, or something, right?"

"You would." Dr. Cavanni tapped her pen thoughtfully against her notebook. "Ever heard of coding boot camp?"

***

Coding boot camp. Trysta liked the sound of it. It sounded...tough. Strong. Demanding. All the things that Trysta had been trained not to be. Like something her father, the ex-Marine, would never approve of for his daughter any more than he approved of anything else she ever did.

But this wasn't her father's boot camp. This was boot camp not for her body but for her brain, and if her brain could take it, if her mind was strong enough to get her through it, then she wouldn't need a father or a husband or a boyfriend or any man to tell her what to be ever again. Trysta would be her own person doing whatever she wanted to do, even if she hadn't quite yet figured out who that person was or what she wanted to do. But in the meantime she'd show them all what Trysta Wells knew how to do with a parabola. Or with a line of computer code.

After she set Miri down for her nap Trysta turned on the desktop computer in the family room and pulled up the information page for Philadelphia Community College. PCC was as good a place to start looking as any, Laura had told her. Trysta scanned the course offerings and in fact found a coding boot camp program. Six months. Ninety-five percent job placement among graduates. Tuition: five thousand dollars. A one hundred fifty dollar fee for the application process, which included a preliminary entrance exam to determine computer proficiency. There was a page of sample code problems. The problems were easier than what she'd had to figure out for Jeremy back in high school. Loans available for living expenses. Work-study options. Student health care available.

Trysta sat back in the desk chair and pulled in a deep breath. She closed her eyes. *Was she going to do this?* Miri began squalling, up too soon from her nap, and now she'd be cranky for the rest of the afternoon. *Oh, yes,* she thought, pulling herself up from the chair, *I am.*

***

Darren spent most of the day at Highland and Erskerberg trying to untangle a commercial real estate contract that had been considerably balled up by the sloppy lawyer of an important client.

Perhaps Darren devoted more time than the client would have expected or his company would have required, smoothing out every small wrinkle of the situation, gilding the lily, making sure that all parties were beyond satisfied. But in truth Darren was desperate, now more than ever, for the Highland and Erskerberg powers that be to consider him an invaluable asset, one that big clients asked for by name to handle their property issues, one that Jeremy Andrews would never again consider letting go of even if Angelo Barbieri told him to.

***

At four o'clock that afternoon Highland and Erskerberg Operations Manager Ellie Krillman sat at her desk staring intently at her computer screen. The knock on her door made her jump, but it was only Darren Miller, swinging by to give her the run-down on the mess from hell she'd assigned him to clean up.

"Can I go, Ellie?" Darren asked after they'd gone over the revised contract, which in Ellie's estimation Darren had done a heroic job of salvaging.

"Go," said Ellie. She looked up from her computer. "You coming in tomorrow?"

"You need me? I was gonna work from home."

"You could. Unless we have any mopping up left on this," she waved her hand at her computer screen, "effed-up crap-a-rama."

Darren laughed. "Jesus, Ellie, you're worse than me. But I think I got it all."

"Yeah I think you did. In that case I won't need you here until the nine AM team meeting the day after tomorrow."

"I'll be here." *I hope,* he added to himself.

After Darren left her office Ellie Krillman sighed and shook her head. With all the stress she had to deal with these days Darren Miller at least was a bright spot. The guy was smart and dependable and always got the job done, though how smart he was in his personal life was highly debatable. Still, Ellie figured that whatever extra-curricular drama Darren might have going on outside the work place was his business so long as it *stayed* outside the workplace. It still rankled her that she'd been required to fire Darren Miller over what she suspected was some sort of sexual triangulation involving himself, Jeremy Andrews and that goofy blonde Betty Boop of a receptionist who was now Darren's wife. Personally Ellie didn't give a rat's rear about Miller's relationship status, he was a damn good real estate broker and she was glad to have him back on her team even if she'd felt like an ass for having to re-hire him as a contractor after she'd just fired him, not on her own authority, as such a personnel action should have been, but at the beck and call of Jeremy Andrews.

But at this point all that was small stuff, and Jeremy Andrews using her to jerk Darren Miller around was the least of her problems with that man. Ellie put her head in her hands. Why the hell was she in this mess? She'd searched her soul trying to figure out whether it was her personal aggravation over Jeremy Andrews that had pushed her to blow the whistle on him to the authorities, but really, what choice had she had? She was Operations Manager and she'd been at Highland and Erskerberg for a good twenty-five years before Jeremy Andrews came strutting in from that high-end Manhattan firm in all his glory and slid into the job of Chief of Global Acquisitions, a job that by rights should have gone to her, and if he thought he was playing her for a fool on the doctored financial reports he was trying to palm off…God, he'd asked her out for dinner, even, a *date*, for crying out loud, Mr. Handsome Samson, a good fifteen years younger than her, did he think he could seduce her into silence, the sexist pig? Buy her loyalty, her complicity, with his smooth charm, bedroom eyes and an expensive dinner even while he was *shtupping* Betty Boop?

Damn, why the hell had she gotten sucked into this position? As far as she knew nobody else in the company, including Jeremy Andrews, knew that she knew that something fishy was going on. But if it had been caught by an auditor or a savvy IRS agent…Well, there was a risk in blowing the whistle and a risk in failing to do so, and so Ellie had made her choice and now here she was, spying on Jeremy Andrews for the FBI, a bundle of nerves inside, losing sleep, losing weight, even, because her stomach was in such a knot. Huh, she thought wryly, finally a diet that works.

***

Darren pulled his car into the in the back lot of Angelo Barbieri's salvage yard. He saw a sleek, shiny new silver-grey Jaguar parked at the corner of the lot. *Good God,* he thought, *don't tell me that dick-head blew the whole wad already.* Darren pulled up alongside the car to see that it was indeed Geoffry sitting in the driver's seat fiddling with his iPhone. *This is it,* Darren thought as he exited his car and hoped he could pull off the performance of his life.

"Aw man, that was easy as fuck," said Geoffry as Darren climbed into the passenger seat of Geoffry's new car. "I got the whole deal done in three days."

"So show me what you bought," said Darren.

"What I bought? This sweet ride, for one thing." Geoffry patted the stitched-leather steering wheel. "Cost me eighty thou. What do you think, Little Bro?"

"Nice," said Darren. His throat was dry with nerves. "I mean what did you buy for Angelo? Out in Wedgefield?"

"Aw, I found this burned-out little piece of shit for eighteen thousand."

"*Eighteen thousand?* What the hell did you get for eighteen thousand? A dog house?"

"I told you. A burned-out piece of shit. Half of a burned-out piece of shit duplex out on East 34th Street."

"East 34th Street? Aw, no way!" Darren felt a thrill dread and glee. His step-brother had outdone himself in stupidity and greed; now if Darren could just lure him along to go the final distance. "I mean," Darren continued, "that's great! Angelo's gonna love it, he'll be able to flip it for a bundle, especially with how those neighborhoods around there are all going gentrified. Yeah, Angelo'll be real happy. You did good, Big Bro." *Hell will gentrify before East 34th Street does, and you just stuck Angelo Barbieri with a worthless liability in a heroin war zone and blew eighty thousand dollars of his money on a Jaguar. He'll be so happy he might rip both our hearts out.*

"Hell, yeah, I did, good," said Geoffry, sounding and looking sublimely pleased with himself. "And I didn't even have to drive out to that shithole neighborhood to look at it. I saw the picture online and I bought it online."

"You *bought* it online?"

"I did it all online. I didn't even have to talk to the guy."

"The guy?"

"The real estate agent. I paid him on PayPal."

"*PayPal*? You bought the property on...*PayPal*?"

Geoffry's eyes narrowed. "What, you think there's something wrong?"

"No, no, I just...How did you do that?"

"What, you don't even know how to buy a property on PayPal, Mr. Big-Shit Real Estate Agent?"

"Well, I..."

"Well, you don't know, right?"

"Fine, I don't." Darren made a conscious effort to sound annoyed. "So how *did* you do it?"

"Think I'm telling you, Dickwad?"

"Okay, fine, don't tell me." Now Darren tried to sound pouty. "I can figure it out on my own. I just wanted to know in case Angelo asked me about it. Speaking of Angelo, give me the deed to the property so I can give it to Angelo and get my pat on the back. He might even throw little something extra my way like he sometimes does when he's happy. You printed off the deed, right?"

"Yeah, I printed off the deed."

"You got it here?"

"Yeah, I got it here." Geoffry reached behind him and grabbed a manila envelope that had been lying on the back seat. He held it away from Darren.

"So are you gonna give it to me?"

"Why should I give it to you?"

"What do you mean why should you give it to me? So I can give it to Angelo."

"You're not giving it to Angelo. I am."

"No you're not! This is *my* deal, right?" Darren reached for the envelope in Geoffry's hand but Geoffry jerked the envelope away, as if he were playing keep-away from Darren.

"Nope," Geoffry snickered, "it's my deal. *I* did all the work."

"Yeah, but I paid you for it," Darren whined. "You got the money, I get the credit."

Geoffry held the envelope out to Darren then again pulled it away when Darren reached for it. "No, *I* get the money and *I* get the credit," said Geoffry. "I'm giving the deed to Angelo and I'm gonna tell him who did all the work. And I'm gonna tell him how you were gonna blow the job off because you don't give a shit and can't handle it anymore. Just like you said."

"Aw, come on, I never said I couldn't handle it! Geoffry, don't be a dick, give me the deed!"

"We'll see who Angelo calls a plank and blows it out his ass on!"

"Shit, man, don't do this! You're gonna get me fired!"

"You're breaking my heart, little Bro. Hey are you crying? Just like when I used to kick your ass when you were a little pussy?"

"No, I'm not...I'm not..." Darren covered his face with one hand and began sniffling loudly.

Geoffry laughed. "Aw get your pussy ass outta my Jag before you get tears on the upholstery."

Darren exited Geoffry's car and slammed the door then stomped back to his car just as he'd stomped off to his room so many times back when he was young and helpless against Geoffry's tormenting. But this time his tears were fake and the rest theatrics just to enhance the act he'd been putting on with Geoffry. Darren slammed his car door and for a finale peeled his car out of the parking lot, in which he could see in his rearview mirror behind him Geoffry standing by his new Jaguar, envelope in hand, laughing.

Act one couldn't have gone better. Darren decided to pull over somewhere and wait for act two.

***

Angelo Barbieri's secretary Dina gasped at the sound of footsteps pounding down the fire exit and jumped up from her desk at the sight of Angelo chasing Geoffry past her desk and out the door. Geoffry had a swollen, blackening eye and blood streamed from his nose. Angelo, without even a jacket against the chilly March air, chased Geoffry out the door and into the parking lot until Geoffry slipped on a patch of gravel and fell backwards, landing on his seat.

"Where you think you're running to, huh?" Angelo said breathlessly. He smacked Geoffry on the top of the head, the only spot he could hit as Geoffry had curled himself into a ball.

"Darren made me do it," Geoffry wailed.

"Yeah, well, Darren's dead, so you don't listen to him anymore, you hear?" Angelo paused a moment to catch his breath. "You dumb shit-for-brains!" He gave Geoffry a kick. "Get up!" After Geoffry was on his feet Angelo pushed him across the parking lot to the Jaguar. "This is what you spent my money on?" he shouted, "A fuckin' *Jaguar?*"

Geoffry was blubbering too hard to answer.

"Well, guess what, Einstein, you're gonna work that money off for me, you understand? You work for me and you get nothing until I say you do, you hear me?" Anglo slapped Geoffry's cheek. "You hear me?"

Geoffry nodded.

"And you don't listen to that punk brother of yours, you got that?"

Geoffry nodded again.

"Now get outta here. Have your ass back here tomorrow."

Geoffry wiped his eyes and reached into his pocket for his keys.

"Gimme those keys." Angelo grabbed the key chain from Geoffry's hands, detached the car key then shoved the key chain at Geoffry. "Where's the title?"

Geoffry looked bewildered. "What?"

Angelo grabbed Geoffry by the collar. "The title, asshole, where is it?"

"At home," Geoffry sobbed.

"You bring me that title, don't show up tomorrow without it if you value your cock and nuts, you hear me?"

Geoffry nodded.

"Now get the hell outta here!" Angelo gave Geoffry a shove for good measure.

"Bu-but...How'm I gonna get home?"

"I don't give a fuck how you get home!" Angelo shook his head. "Oh for Christ's sake, call a fuckin' Uber, you idiot!"

***

112

Angelo smacked the intercom button outside the door of his building. "Buzz me in, Dina, I don't have my goddamn key."

Dina buzzed her boss back into the building. "Is everything all right, Mr. Barbieri?" she asked as Angelo huffed by her desk, a dark scowl on his face.

"Call my wife," he called back over his shoulder, "Tell her she got her fuckin' Jaguar."

***

Darren sat in the parking lot of a fast food restaurant off the Schuylkill Expressway holding, but otherwise ignoring, the coffee he'd bought at the drive-thru.

"No," he practiced saying to an imaginary Angelo Barbieri, "no, I'm not coming back...I quit...Fuck you, Angelo, I quit! I *quit*, Angelo...I'm just...I'm not coming back, Angelo... Hey, I'm sorry that Geoffry screwed up, I tried to tell him...I just wanted to give him a chance...No, I quit...Go ahead, call Jeremy Andrews, I quit... No...No...No...NO...NO...NO! Go ahead and break my legs, I QUIT!"

Darren turned his head to see an elderly man and woman a few feet away from his car, staring at him. He smiled, toasted them with his coffee cup then took a sip. The couple moved on, turning back to glance at him on their way into the restaurant. *Jesus.* Darren prayed that Angelo would fire him, just outright fire him. Despite the cool temperature he was sweating. His heart was pounding.

He waited another five minutes for his phone to ring then jumped when it did. He looked at the name on the screen and felt a stomach-turning thrill of dread. He closed his eyes. *Gotta do this, gotta do this.* He pulled in a deep breath then answered the inevitable. "Hello?"

"Don't 'hello' me, you little prick!" Angelo shouted into his ear. "What the hell's going on? I give you a hundred and ten thousand dollars and you give it to that *oobatz* brother of yours? What the fuck?"

Darren recited the script he'd rehearsed for this moment. "Hey, it was you who said I should take Geoffry onboard, work as a team, right? *I due fratelli.* You said it, remember?" *Fire me,* Darren thought.

"*I due* assholes!"

"I mean, is it my fault he got confused? I told him 'just don't buy some cheap piece of shit out in Wedgefield.' Is it my fault all he heard was 'buy some cheap piece of shit out in Wedgefield?' Did I tell him to go buy a Jaguar with the change?" *Now fire me.*

"You lying fuck!"

"I swear, Angelo! I was just trying to give Geoffry a chance. Look, ever since I started here Geoffry's been harboring this, this *resentment*, and I was just trying to"

"*Resentment?*" Angelo cut him off, "I'll shove his resentment up his ass and yours, too!"

"Hey I'm sorry Geoffry screwed up. *I* screwed up. I screwed up big time, I admit it." *Fire me.*

"Shut up, you moron!"

"I mean, if you wanna fire me," said Darren, talking faster and sounding contrite, "you should. Go ahead, fire me, I fucked up. I deserve it. Fire me." *Please! Fire me now!*

There was a moment of silence on Angelo's end. "*Fire* you? You want me to *fire* you?"

"Well," Darren drove on, "I mean, I deserve it, and all."

"Is that what this bullshit is all about? You're tryna get me to *fire* you?"

Darren felt his heart sinking. "No, I mean, I don't want you to, but"

"Yeah, I'll fire you all right! I'll fire you from that cushy little gig you got over at Highland and Erskerberg, I'll get you fired today! Tomorrow you'll be cleaning out your desk and taking home your window plant, Bobby D. Here, you wanna listen while I call Jeremy Andrews?"

"No," said Darren dejectedly. It had been too much to hope for that he'd still have the Highland and Erskerberg job before this was over. "So I'm fired. Okay. I gotta go."

"Wait, wait, wait, Bobby D., where you gotta go? To get your ass in gear and dump that piece of crap you sent your idiot brother to buy out in Wedgefield? That better be where you're going, because you're gonna take care of that and get me back my hundred and ten grand, that's on *you*, you hear me? You get me my money! *Fire* you?" Angelo laughed. "In your dreams Bobby D." There was an unveiled threat in Angelo Barbieri's voice. "From now on your ass belongs to me, not to

Highland and Erskerberg and not even to that *succose* little cannoli you got waiting in the bedroom for you at home. From now on you belong to me and you work for me and me only, you got that, Bobby D.?"

Darren's resolve suddenly melted away like cotton candy, dissolved in his fear and resignation that he could never stand up to Angelo Barbieri and could no more escape him than a fly could escape the sticky glue entrapping it in a spider's web.

"Hey, what's the matter, D.? Pussy got your tongue? You understand what I said?"

Darren felt a stray tear of despair roll down his cheek. "Yeah." *No.*

"Come by tomorrow, D., Okay? You understand me?"

"Yeah." *No. No, no, no, NO! NO!* "No!" Darren shouted into the phone, "NO!"

"What? What did I hear you say?"

"No! I'm not coming back! I'm finished with you, Angelo! I quit!"

"You quit? My ass you quit! You don't quit me, you punk, not when you owe me a hundred and ten grand! Who the fuck you think you are?"

Calm down, Darren instructed himself, pulling in another deep breath. *Think. Say it.* "I'll get you back your money. I swear I will."

"You bet your ass you will!"

"I will. I'm good for it. I just gotta…sell a house. But I'm not working for you anymore. I'm done."

"You're *done?"* Angelo's voice sounded high-pitched with rage. "You think you're fuckin' *done?* You know who I *know?* You know what I can *do* to you?"

Suddenly the image flashed into Darren's mind of Angelo, sitting in his swanky-looking office over his run-down salvage yard, screaming himself red in the face into his phone, screaming himself hoarse, maybe screaming himself into a heart attack. *If he could really do anything else to you,* said a voice in his head, *why would he have to scream?* "I'm done," Darren said calmly.

"Yeah, you're done, you little cunt, you're one hundred percent done! You're gonna hear a knock at your front door, you hear me, *Bobby Cunt Darren?* And when you hear that knock you better tell your cunt wife and your cunt kids to go hide upstairs in the bedroom closet! Yeah, you're done!" Then there was silence.

Darren looked at his cell phone. It was over. He breathed a deep breath of relief. Whatever came next, for better or worse, he was free at last from Angelo Barbieri.

***

Ellie Krillman was packing in her day, thinking about what she'd eat for dinner that night and, now that the mess with the client's lawyer was mopped up, whether she'd find herself a few minutes tonight to watch some Netflix, take her mind off the Jeremy Andrews drama-rama. She was putting on her coat when her phone rang. "Aw, *crap*," she muttered, then answered, "What can I do for you Jeremy?" Ellie's eyes widened in disbelief. "You want me to...*fire Darren Miller?*" She listened while Jeremy spouted what she figured to be some hogwash about poor quarterly numbers. "But I just hired him back. What am I supposed to tell him this time?"

"Poor quarterlies," said Jeremy, then he hung up.

"Aw, gimme a *break*," Ellie said as she stared at her phone screen. She sat down at her desk and held her phone in one hand, tapping her fingers on her desk top with the other. *Oh, Darren, Darren*, she thought, *you're up to your eyeballs in something*. She pulled up a number on her phone, cancelled it, pulled it up again, cancelled it again. *Who am I kidding*, she thought. *Sorry*, Darren, *I have to do this*.

Then she cancelled the number again and looked at the screen. *But do I have to do it this minute?*

Chapter Twelve

By evening the relief Darren had felt that afternoon as he'd hung up on Angelo Barbieri had been punctured and deflated by sharp prickles of anxiety.

He sat at the dinner table absently poking at his food, tuned out from the usual background racket of Trysta's kids and even from baby Silvia Miri whom he reflexively bounced in his lap.

By tomorrow he'd be out of a job at Highland and Erskerberg. Would security meet him at the door and bar his entrance to the building? Or would they allow him to clean out his desk before escorting him out, as they'd done last time they'd fired him?

And what had Barbieri meant about a knock at his door? That was just bullshit, right? Barbieri wouldn't risk having me...having me ...my fingerprints are all over his business...but what has he ever let me see besides the shady little money-laundering deals he has me doing? I didn't lose him that much money that he'd have me...have me ...and if he sent somebody to, to... I'd call the police, I'd testify, I'd, I'd, I'd end up getting in trouble myself if I called the police, and Barbieri knows it, but would he really...send somebody...somebodies...to my house? What would they do to Trysta? The kids? The baby? No, Barbieri wouldn't

Darren gasped at the sound of the loud knock at the front door.

"Now, who's that?" said Trysta.

"And why are knocking?" asked Trina. "Don't they even know how to ring the *doorbell?*"

"Yeah, don't they even know how to ring the *doorbell?*" echoed Sam.

"Maybe the stupid bell is broken," said Zach.

"It's not *stupid*," said Trina.

"No, *you* are," said Zach.

"*Mo-om!*" wailed Trina.

"Well, are you gonna get it, Darren?" asked Trysta.

But Darren sat paralyzed with fear. "I think they're gone," he said, his voice quivering just above a whisper.

There were several more loud knocks.

"Aaaah!" Darren sprung from his chair.

"What's the matter?" asked Trysta.

"Everybody! Run upstairs! Hide in the closet! Here, Trysta, take the baby! And keep her quiet! Everybody be quiet!"

"Darren, *what...?*" cried Trysta as Darren pushed Silvia Miri into her arms.

"Just *do it* Trysta!" cried Darren, herding her and the children from the kitchen down the hallway to the stairs while the knocking persisted.

"And shut up," said Zach as he dragged his wailing sisters. Rising to the occasion, Zach had taken it upon himself to help Darren shepherd his family out of whatever harm's way they were now in.

"That's right, Zach," said Darren, "get 'em all upstairs, hide them somewhere, in a closet, and *be quiet!*"

"Come on you guys," said Zach, pushing his mother and sisters up the stairs. "Mom, make the baby stop crying!"

"Mommy, give her some *milk!*" sobbed Trina.

"Mommy, give her some *milk!*" sobbed Sam.

Trysta fumbled to put the baby on her breast while hurrying up the stairs. "For God's sake, Darren," she called down from the top of the stairs, "why don't you call the po"

"Mom!" cried Zach, pulling his mother's arm, "Get in the bedroom closet! *Now!*"

"Hey, somebody in there?" called a deep, slightly accented male voice from the other side of the front door.

Darren's heart began racing. Fuck, Trysta and the kids had probably sounded like a herd of wailing elephants through this cheap-assed door on this cheaply-constructed piece of shit over-priced house...why hadn't he just let them stay in the kitchen and told them to be quiet? Darren peeked through the front door peephole. He saw a man in a black coat. Looked Mexican, or something. Darren broke into a sweat. From next to the man he saw a dark-skinned fist rise towards the door. He jumped at the sound of the fist hitting the door.

"Hey, anybody?" called the Mexican.

Darren turned around and leaned against the door. Dear Jesus, what should he do? Go up and hide with the others? Yes. But what if they broke in? He should call the police. And tell them…what? That two men were at his door and he was afraid they were going to kill him? How could he tell them what he was afraid of without getting himself arrested for his dealings with Angelo Barbieri? Another round of pounding. Jesus, he wished to God it was the police! He'd confess everything! In fact, if he got out of this alive he'd go to the authorities and confess *everything!*

But he had to do something. *Now.* He had to. He had to. Do something. *Anything.* He felt faint. *Oh, Jesus, save me!* He prayed as he turned around and faced the door. He sucked in a deep breath and yelled, *"Get the fuck out of here, you pieces of shit, before I blow you both away!"*

Silence on the other side of the door. He thought he could hear the sound of feet running down the walkway. Oh, God, had it worked? Were they gone? Had he actually scared off Barbieri's goons?

Darren pulled in several great gulps of air. *Calm down,* he counseled himself, *breathe.* What to do now? What if they came back? What if they came back with more of them? What if they were still outside, waiting for Darren to open the door? What if they came back to ambush Darren in the morning when he left for work? What if they decided to wait a day or two, catch Darren off guard…but they'd be back, and probably soon, to get the job done.

The minutes passed but Darren was afraid to move. Off in the distance he could hear police sirens. He wished they were on their way to this neighborhood. The sirens sounded as if they were getting closer and closer until they seemed to be on his street.

Darren tiptoed to the living room window and through the slats of the blinds he saw flashing red and blue lights. *The police were here! At his house! Somehow they knew!*

"Trysta! Kids!" he called up the stairs, "It's all right! Come down! The police are here!"

His heart brimming with relief and gratitude, Darren pulled open his front door to find himself facing a semi-circle of half-a-dozen SWAT officers on the walk in front of his porch, the barrels of their assault rifles pointed at his head. Behind them were a line of police officers aiming pistols at him from behind the cover of the hoods of their vehicles. Among the police vehicles parked on his street was an armored personnel carrier.

"Step outside and put your hands up!" commanded a voice through a megaphone.

Darren stood in the doorway dumbly frozen in drop-jawed, wide-eyed bewilderment.

"STEP...OUT...SIDE...AND...PUT... YOUR... HANDS... *UP!*" demanded the megaphone as the assault rifles took a step closer.

Darren slowly raised his hands and stepped outside.

"Come off the porch and step onto the walk then stop," ordered the megaphone. "Anyone else inside the house, come out with your hands up,"

While Darren obeyed the megaphone's instructions, out the front door and onto the front porch stepped Trysta, one hand raised, the other holding her baby. Her two small daughters and Zach, hands raised, stepped close beside her.

The megaphone gave an audible sigh. "Okay, everybody put your hands down. Anybody else in the house?" The little group shook their heads.

"You folks okay?" asked the megaphone.

Darren, hands still in the air, glanced over his shoulder at his family. "Yeah," he said breathlessly, "yeah, we're okay."

"Sir, you can lower your hands," said the megaphone, sounding slightly exasperated. The SWAT team leader standing in front of the armored personnel carrier lowered the megaphone and took in the sight of the frightened family shivering in the night air. To the police officer standing next to him he muttered, "Pork me in the ear with your left toe if this isn't another bullshit run." Then he called to his team and the police officers around him, "Okay, everybody lower your weapons." He headed up the driveway followed by the regular police officers.

"What's going on here?" the SWAT team leader asked Darren.

"The two guys, they must have got away," said Darren.

The SWAT team members and police officers looked at each other. "What two guys?" asked the SWAT leader.

Darren gasped as the Hispanic man in the black coat exited one of the police cars followed by a tall, solidly-built black...*woman.*

"Them!" cried Darren, pointing to the two, now heading up the driveway, "those two...people."

The SWAT leader looked over his shoulder. *"Them?"* he asked incredulously. "Buddy, you know who they *are?*"

The SWAT leader stood back in deference as the man and the woman approached Darren. Both held up badges.

"Robbi Downer, Federal Bureau of Investigation," said the woman.

"Miggy Corazón, Internal Revenue Service," said the man. Darren noticed that the man carried an official-looking bound black notebook.

Darren began to laugh breathlessly, uncontrollably, "You're, you're...? You're not, not....?"

"Bad guys?" finished Zach for Darren, who was laughing too hard to speak.

"Bad guys?" asked Agent Corazón, glancing at Agent Downer.

Agent Downer asked, "Was it you told us to..." she glanced at Trysta and the children, "...buzz off and threatened to blow us away?"

"Well...yeah...yeah," laughed Darren, gasping for breath, his face red with the exertion, "but...I..."

"Guy's hysterical," Agent Corazón whispered to the SWAT team leader.

The SWAT leader nodded and stepped forward. "You know it's a Federal offense to threaten a Federal agent? Carries a sentence of up to ten years?" The Swat leader looked briefly over his shoulder and winked at the IRS agent.

Darren's laughter stopped with a gasp and the color drained from his face. He pulled in several deep gulps of air to keep from fainting.

"Don't you dare! Don't you *dare!*"

Darren looked over his shoulder to see Trysta, her face aflame, stomping down the porch steps followed by Zach and the girls.

"Mo-om!" cried Zach.

"Mommy!" sobbed Trina and Sam.

"Trysta, what are you"

"Here," she cut Darren off, shoving wailing Silvia Miri into his arms. Then she stepped up to the confounded agents. "How *dare* you!" she cried.

"Trysta, don't"

"Shut up, Darren! Shut up children! For once everybody just shut up and *listen to me! Everybody!*"

Stunned by this strange new incarnation of their wife and mother, Darren, the children, even little Silvia Miri, obeyed her command. The police officers, unsure of what the situation warranted, awaited further instruction and raised their weapons slightly, their fingers close to the triggers.

FBI Agent Robbi Downer raised her hand to the police officers. "Go ahead, M'am. Everybody's listening."

Now that she'd grabbed the moment, Trysta looked unsure as to what she should do with it. She cleared her throat. "Well," she began, "I mean, we're all just sitting around the kitchen table having a nice family dinner, and *you* start pounding on our door and yelling and scaring us all to *death.*"

"And you should of rung the doorbell," piped up little Sam.

"Shhh," said Zach.

"Uh, we tried your doorbell," said Agent Miggy Corazón. "It fell off the wall when I pushed it. See? There it is lying on the porch."

Trysta looked back at the porch. "Oh. Well, you still didn't have to scare us all to death."

"Daddy Darren made us run upstairs and hide in the closet, and we were all crying, even Mommy and Zach," said Sam, still sniffling.

"I was *not,*" said Zach, wiping his eyes and giving his sister a light shove.

"Oh, so *that* was all the running around and crying we heard inside the house," said Agent Downer. "You were running upstairs to *hide?*"

"We thought there was trouble going on inside," said Agent Corazón. "And then when this guy threatened to blow us away…"

"Yeah, sorry about that," said Darren. "I thought you were…"

"Wait…Why *were* you all so afraid of a knock on the door?" asked Agent Downer.

"We weren't afraid," said Trina, "Mommy said, 'Darren, go answer the door,' and Daddy Darren made us all run upstairs and *then* we got all upset and started crying."

Darren chuckled nervously. "Heh, heh, well, you know, all the gangs you hear about these days, breaking into people's houses, and all the crazy shooters, heh, heh."

"Oh," said Agent Downer. "We apologize for the trouble."

"*Crazy shooters?*" whispered one police officer to another.

"*Thank* you," sniffed Trysta. "Now if you don't mind, the children are freezing," she took the baby from Darren, "and we need to go back inside."

"Take the children back inside, M'am," said Agent Downer.

"We finished here?" asked the SWAT team leader.

"Yeah," said Agent Downer with a wave of her hand, then she called to the departing SWAT and police officers, "Thanks for coming, ladies and gentlemen, sorry for your trouble."

There was a general mumbling among the departing group. "I wish to hell they'd put me back in South Philly," said one SWAT officer to another, "these rich suburban types are nuts."

As Darren turned to follow his wife into the house Agent Downer said, "Darren Miller?"

Darren's stomach flipped as he turned back.

"Agent Corazón and I, we came by to ask you a few questions."

Darren's heart began racing again. "Questions?" he croaked.

"Yeah, that's why we came by," said Agent Corazón. "To ask you a couple of questions."

"About, uh, what?"

"About your work."

"My…*work?*" The word "*work*" came out as a squeak.

"Can we come inside?" asked Agent Downer.

"Uh, well, uh," Darren stammered, "I mean, my wife, the kids, and all…"

"Okay. Maybe now isn't a good time…?" Agent Corazón glanced at his colleague, who nodded.

"Yes, please come back another time," Trysta called tersely from the front door. "And next time please call before you come. Darren, come inside. Now."

"Yeah, right," said Darren, "maybe another time. Sorry for the confusion, and all, but, uh, yeah, well, another time. I'm just gonna… " Darren pointed towards his house then turned and began walking away from the agents, his heart still hammering in his chest.

"Mr. Miller," called Agent Downer.

Darren turned to see the two agents following him up the walk. Agent Downer held out a card.

"Why don't you just come and talk to us downtown when you're ready. Here's the address. Phone number. Give me a call before you come. Call any time."

"Oh," said Darren. "So…you want me to come downtown…to…"

"Like we said, we just have some questions," said Agent Corazón.

"About your work," added Agent Downer.

"Well, uh," Darren chuckled nervously, "I'm kind of busy, so if I don't, I mean, if I can't get there right away…"

"Then we'll be back," said Agent Downer. "Good night, Mr. Miller. And I suggest you get that doorbell fixed."

Darren watched as the two agents headed down the walk to their car. *They'll be back,* the words pounded in his ears, *they'll be back, they'll be back, they'll be back…*

"Wait!" Darren called, running down the walk. The agents stopped. "Wait," he said, breathlessly, "wait. I can't do this anymore. I'll tell you everything."

The agents exchanged a look. Agent Downer said, "You'll tell us…everything?"

"Everything," said Darren, "everything."

Robbi Downer and Miggy Corazón followed Darren into the house, shrugging and shaking their heads behind his back.

"Darren, what in the world is going on?" asked Trysta, following Darren and the agents down the hallway and into his office with the baby in her arms and the children close behind her.

"I'm telling them everything," said Darren.

"Everything....*what?*" said Trysta.

"You take the kids, go finish dinner."

"Darren, are you *kidding* me? No, I'm staying right here. I want to hear everything, too."

"We want to hear everything, too!" cried Trina.

"Yeah, we want to hear everything, too!" echoed Sam.

"No you don't," snapped Zach, "get back in the kitchen and eat your dinner. Mom, give me the baby. Come on, you guys." Zach took Silvia Miri and ushered his protesting sisters back into the kitchen.

***

Darren closed the door to his office. "Sorry, I guess I don't have enough seats."

"You and Mrs. Miller sit," said Agent Robbi Downer. "We'll stand. Bear in mind that while this interview is totally voluntary, Title Eighteen, United States Code, Section One Thousand and One makes it a federal felony to lie to a federal officer in the performance of his or her official duties."

Miggy Corazón flipped open his notebook and pulled out a pen.

"Okay," Darren whispered hoarsely. He pulled in a deep breath and without waiting to be questioned he began talking, telling them everything.

***

Darren rubbed his eyes and his temples "So that's it," he said, "everything. Today Barbieri let me go, tomorrow...I don't know what'll happen when I walk into Highland and Erskerberg."

Robbi Downer looked pensive. Miggy Corazón spent a moment looking over the notes he'd taken, then he looked up at Darren. "And just now you thought we were a couple of Angelo Barbieri's...people?"

"Yeah," said Darren.

"So basically," said Agent Downer, "Barbieri has you buying and selling real estate for him and maintaining a bank account while your step-bother Geoffry Steubing signs his checks and helps you? Or did before you quit Barbieri?"

"Yeah," Darren sighed. He turned to Trysta, who'd sat quietly gnawing her lip and nails during the interview until she sprang up from her seat when Darren mentioned that it was Highland and Erskerberg executive Jeremy Andrews who'd re-hired him and would now re-fire him at Angelo Barbieri's bidding. "And now you know everything, too," he said to Trysta. She sat back down and covered her face with her hands, shaking her head.

"Am I under arrest?" Darren asked miserably. Trysta sobbed softly from behind her hands.

The two agents looked at each other. "Mr. Miller," said Agent Downer, "we didn't come here to arrest you. We didn't even come here to ask about Angelo Barbieri. The guy's been low on our radar for years, but up until now we've never been able to peg anything on him. We had no idea you were tied up with him. Now that you've told us what you've told us, could we make a case against you? Eh, if we really wanted to. But I don't think we really want to," Miggy Corazón nodded his head in agreement, "because you talked to us voluntarily and you're far more valuable to us as a witness."

"No," gasped Trysta.

"I meant as a source," Agent Downer clarified. "Don't worry, we'll make sure Barbieri never finds out you talked to us. He probably believes you're as compromised as he is. He'll likely try to pin any illegal actions on you and your step-brother. In any case, as far as we know, Barbieri doesn't really have any hard mob connections. As far as we know. At best we figured he might be doing a little laundering for them. We never thought of Barbieri as such a big fish."

"You think he is now?" asked Darren.

"Not sure," said agent Downer. "But we're gonna find out. What you've told us seems to point to…something."

"Tax fraud, at least," added Agent Corazón. "And money laundering."

"What about threatening Darren and me and the children?" asked Trysta. "Can't you arrest him for that?"

"That one might be a little trickier to pin on him," said Agent Downer. "I believe our best bet is gonna be to follow the money."

"Will Darren have to testify? In court?" asked Trysta.

"Nah," said Agent Corazón. "We don't need courtroom testimony. Just evidence. Either we'll find it or we won't. If we find it, that'll be all we need."

"And if you don't?" asked Darren.

"Oh, if it's there, we'll find it, all right," said Agent Downer.

"We're gonna need access to any bank accounts you opened for Barbieri," said Agent Corazón.

"Oh sure, sure," said Darren. "You don't know what a relief it is to get rid of all this, this… garbage."

"Huh," muttered Trysta from behind her hands.

"Speaking of garbage," Agent Corazón muttered to his partner.

"Right," said Agent Downer. To Darren she said, "So we appreciate your cooperation regarding Angelo Barbieri. But as I said, we didn't come here to ask you about him."

Trysta looked up from behind her hands. Her eyes were reddened and wet with tears. "What *did* you come here for?" she asked.

"Mr. Miller," continued Agent Downer, "have you told us everything you have to tell us about Jeremy Andrews?"

Trysta once again sprung up and began pacing.

Darren's eyes followed his wife's pacing. "Huh? Jeremy Andrews?"

"The head of Global Acquisitions?" said Agent Downer, "the guy who fired you then re-hired you and who Barbieri threatened to have fire you again?"

"Oh, yeah, yeah," said Darren, "that's all I know about him. I mean, it seems like Angelo Barbieri is pulling his strings somehow, but I don't know how." Then Darren added, "Only it wasn't Jeremy Andrews who fired me from Highland and Erskerberg that first time, I was let go because the company was streamlining. He just hired me back after Angelo"

"Yes it was," Trysta cut him off, "It *was* Jeremy who fired you the first time."

Darren gazed dumbly at his wife. Agent Corazón stood with his pen frozen in mid-air over his notebook. Agent Downer blinked several times, cleared her throat, and then asked calmly, "Why do you say that, Mrs. Miller?"

"Because it's true. I know it is. I know a lot of things. And maybe *I* want to tell everything, too."

"Everything…*what?*" said Darren.

"Everything *everything*," said Trysta.

"Go ahead," said Agent Downer.

Trysta sat down and pulled in a deep breath.

***

She told the story of her seduction and then rejection by Jeremy Andrews and all that followed, including his firing of Darren as a scheme to get Trysta out of his sight and mind. She felt like closing her eyes and covering her ears, like she used to do when she was in trouble as a child, before she'd mastered the art of tears and sex appeal; but she just sat with her eyes lowered and waited for the impact of the bomb she'd just dropped on her life.

"Well, okay," said the FBI agent.

"Ummm-hmmm," added the IRS agent, his head bent over his notebook.

Darren, when he finally found his voice, sputtered, "You…he…I don't fuckin'…*That son-of-a-bitch Jeremy Andrews ruined my life!*"

"Yeah," Trysta chuckled bitterly. "Well now you can have it back."

"I'd like to fucking…*Huh?*"

"Your life. You can have it back. I'm leaving you."

"You're *what?*"

"Leaving you. Or you can leave me. That's what you want, right? It's what you're planning, anyway."

"Well…uh…okay, yeah, but…*you* want that, too?"

Trysta nodded.

"Okay, well, all right," Darren chuckled unsurely. "So, I mean, you and the kids…?"

"Silvio wants the children. I'm not fighting him anymore. He can have the children. And you can go ahead and sell the house."

Darren felt as if a great weight had just been lifted from his shoulder. He blew out a deep breath. "Wow, that's... What about Miri?"

Trysta shrugged. "Silvio can have custody of Miri, too, if he wants. If not..." Trysta glanced at the two agents to see if she could read disapproval in their expressions, then decided she didn't care.

"Wait, how could Silvio get custody of Miri? He's not even her father, or step-father, or anything."

Agent Downer opened her mouth to answer Darren's question, then thought better of it and kept her silence.

Trysta shrugged. "I don't know."

"So, like, where will you live? With your parents?"

"Maybe. I don't know yet."

"Wow, this is, I mean..."

"Uh, Okay, Mr. and Mrs. Miller, this has been, uh, very helpful," said Agent Downer.

"Yeah, you've, uh, answered some questions for us," added Agent Corazón.

"What if your parents won't let you move in?" asked Darren, who was now pacing the room.

"Huh," Trysta chuckled bitterly, "You know my parents."

"Uh, actually, not very well. Your father, I mean, he's..."

"He probably won't let me move in. Maybe I can cry him into it. I don't know."

"Well, if there's anybody who can cry her way into it, it's you."

"Mr. and Mrs. Miller," said Agent Downer, "We're gonna go now."

"Yeah," said Trysta, "crying is one thing I can do. I've done enough."

"But we'll be in touch," said Agent Corazón. "And Mr. Miller, I'm gonna be looking into those bank accounts you opened for Angelo Barbieri. I'll need you to give me access. In fact if we could take a minute for you to just give me the account password..."

"Okay, look," said Darren, "We'll sell the house, get the kids settled with Silvio, I'll get a place for me...all right, maybe you could move in with me, you know, just 'til you get yourself, you know, 'til you figure out what you're gonna do, get a job…"

"I'm going back to school."

"School? You?"

"Yes, *me*. I'm going to apply to Philadelphia Community College for coding boot camp. It's six months. I'll get loans. And a job. And student health care."

"Wow," said Darren, still recovering from the shock, "that's, uh…wow."

"But I'll still need a place to live for a while," said Trysta, "so if I could move in with you…"

"Uh, yeah, okay," said Darren. "While you're in school and all."

"Or I could contact you later about the password," said Agent Corazón. "In a day or two."

"We'll let ourselves out," said Agent Downer.

"Okay, I'll move in with you. While I'm at school. Thanks, Darren," said Trysta. "Except I'm not sleeping with you anymore."

"What? Why?"

The two agents stopped in the door way of Darren's office.

"Because I'm gay."

Agents Downer and Corazón stepped back into the room. Robbi Downer closed the door.

"You're *what? Gay?"* Darren chuckled incredulously. "You're kidding, right?"

But Trysta didn't look as if she were kidding. She shook her head. "I'm gay," she said.

"No, you're not fuckin'… *gay!* You fuckin'…you fuckin' *sleep* with me all the time!"

"Hey, buddy," said Miggy, "calm down, okay?"

"I'm gay," said Trysta.

"What the hell?" Darren laughed incredulously, "When did you turn…*gay?* Like, fifteen minutes ago? Oh wait, wait…is this something that happened from that psychologist you've been seeing?"

"The psychologist made her gay?" Miggy Corazón whispered to Robbi Downer.

"No. I've always been gay."

"She's always been gay," Robbi whispered to Miggy.

"You've *always been gay?*" said Darren. "What the hell are you, the world's greatest actor?"

"Yeah," Trysta sighed, "I am. I was gay when I slept with you and when I slept with Silvio and when I slept with Jeremy Andrews." Trysta pulled in a deep breath. *I'm gonna do it,* she thought. "And even when I slept with Jeremy DeCiccio."

"Jeremy *who?*" Robbi whispered to Miggy.

"Jeremy *who?*" Darren looked aghast. "Wait, you were sleeping with *another* guy?"

"Jeremy DeCiccio was my boyfriend back in high school. Who got me pregnant. With Zach. And then dumped me."

"What?" cried Darren. "Did Silvio know about this...Jeremy DeCiccio?"

"What do you want to bet Silvio didn't know about Jeremy DeCiccio?" Miggy whispered to Robbi.

"No," said Trysta. "He thinks he's Zach's father. That's why he married me."

"*Gurrrl,*" whispered Robbi to Miggy.

"You tricked Silvio? You tricked Silvio, you tricked me, you're gay, you sleep with every fuckin' guy who comes along, what the fuck's the *matter* with you, you, you, twisted little *cunt?*"

Trysta flinched as if she'd been hit, her face red and her eyes filled with tears. Miggy Corazon and Robbi Downer each took one of Darren's arms and pulled him back from Trysta. "Mr. Miller, you need to *calm down,*" said Robbi Downer.

"I thought that's what I was supposed to do. Please boys. Please men. I thought it was what I *had* to do. To tell you the truth, it's the only thing I ever really learned to do. I guess I knew or believed deep down that every man I ever loved who said he loved me would eventually throw me away when it stopped being all about sex. So of course I knew I had to make the sex as good as I could. And I could make it good, right?"

Darren shook his head. "Yeah."

"But then all these babies...dumb me, right?"

"Dumb you, dumb me," said Darren.

"But I love them," Trysta sobbed, wiping away with her sleeve the tears that rolled down her cheek, "I love all my babies, I don't care who the fathers are or whether the fathers love them or not. But I can't support them or take care of them right now because I've got to learn how to support myself first. I've got to go back to school, learn how to do something with my life...find out who I'm supposed to be. And I can't do it living here in this house with you and all these children and pretending to be this great sexy wife and this great mother, because..." Trysta was sobbing openly, "The truth is I'm an awful wife and a terrible mother!"

Darren sighed. In spite of himself he wrapped his arms around his sobbing wife. "Look, it's okay, we'll get it all straightened out, okay? We'll call Silvio...All right, don't tell him about Jeremy...DeCoochio, or whatever, okay?"

"Okay," Trysta sniffed.

"Yeah, that'll just be our secret."

"Good call," said Robbi Downer.

Darren looked over at the two agents. "Hey, you guys won't say anything about it, right?"

The agents nodded and said, "Right."

"But anyway we'll call Silvio about taking the kids, and then we can sell the house, and..." Darren looked towards the opening door of his office.

"Are we gonna go live with Daddy now?" asked Trina. She stepped into the office followed by Sam and Zach, who was still holding Silvia Miri.

"Mom, can you take her now?" said Zach as he handed his sister to his mother.

"Sure I will," sniffed Trysta, taking the baby then kissing her head and cooing, "My little precious."

"So, are we gonna go live with Dad?" asked Zach.

Trysta and Darren exchanged a look then Darren said, "Yeah, I think that's gonna be the plan."

"Can we go right now?" asked Zach.

***

On her way out with Agent Corazón Agent Downer stopped and turned to the family, all of whom had followed the two agents to the front door. "I'm going to contact your local police and ask them to put an unmarked car in front of your house for a day or two, so don't be alarmed. We'll have the police contact you about it."

"Okay," said Trysta.

"And Mr. Miller," said agent Corazón, "you be sure and go into Highland and Erskerberg tomorrow. Be there by about, oh, nine-thirty."

"Tomorrow?" asked Darren. "Tomorrow I was planning on doing some work from home, but..."

"Fine," said Robbi Downer, "work from home. Only make sure you're in the office at nine-thirty."

"Uh, okay," said Darren.

"And by the way, Mrs. Miller?"

"What?" said Trysta.

"You raised some nice kids."

***

After the two agents walked down the path from the house to their car in stone-faced silence Miggy pulled the keys from his pocket. "You want me to drive again?" he asked, clicking open the car door locks.

"Sure," said Robbi, opening the passenger's side, "and pull over up the block."

When the car was out of sight of the Miller house Miggy pulled over to the curb. He looked at Robbi who looked back at him. Both agents burst into laughter, laughing themselves to tears.

"Ah, I don't even know what the hell to say about that one," said Miggy, wiping his eyes and pulling back onto the street.

"I'm going home and pouring myself a big glass of wine, and that's all I *even* have to say about it," said Robbi.

"You better make it a small glass," said Miggy. "I believe we are gonna have us a *long* day tomorrow. Land us a big fish. Maybe two."

"And if it turns out to be Angelo Barbieri who's pulling Jeremy Andrews' strings we are gonna land us one very big fish indeed."

Chapter Thirteen

It had been a long day full of broken pipes, backed up sinks and toilets and a root-choked sewer line from hell out on Frankfort Avenue. It was after seven o'clock when Silvio got back to Quick and Reliable from his last job, long after the other guys had finished up and Ida, the efficient, dependable office manager he'd inherited from his Uncle Bud, had closed up shop for the night.

Silvio was dead tired, not so much from the long day as because he hadn't been sleeping well, which hadn't helped the ever-swirling fog in his brain over this whole Silvia paternity thing, which was why he couldn't sleep, so it was a vicious circle, or cycle, or whatever they called it.

And then there was Sally. He'd been neglecting her and he felt guilty about it. But coming to a decision about Silvia and, with Charleston's help, a plan, had helped clear his mind about a lot of things, and now he could see that it wasn't Sally or even himself that was the problem but, as always, Trysta and Darren's antics. He wanted to put right whatever was wrong between himself and Sally. Today he'd had not five free minutes to call her, but he didn't want a quick five minutes anyway. He wanted to really talk to her, from his heart. And now that his brain was clearer things would be better with him and Sally.

Tired as he was, he decided that after he unloaded his work equipment he'd drive over to Sally's house, surprise her, they'd talk, maybe even end up in bed. The thought of bed made him yawn. Well, maybe she'd let him spend the night on the couch.

He'd just pulled out his keys and set the building alarm when his cell rang. It was Trysta. Concerned as always that it might be something about one of his kids, he disarmed the alarm and took the call. It was his kids, all of them on speaker phone. Something about the police. And them coming to live with him. He walked over to the beat-up old leather couch in the far corner of the office and sat down. Then he lay down. Then he sat up.

Twenty minutes later when he hung up the phone his heart was pounding. He knew Charleston would be gone for the night but he called his office anyway and left a message. And he had to tell Sally, right now. He began scrolling down the screen of his phone to her number then stopped. It was almost eight pm. She'd be tucking Josh in right about now, probably reading him a story while she held David on her lap. He'd call her in ten minutes, tell her the crazy, unbelievable, fantastic news. Then, if she wanted him to, he'd drive over there and maybe, after David was down for the night, they'd celebrate.

Silvio lay back down on the sofa and blew out a long sigh. It was as if a ten-ton weight had just been lifted from his shoulders. He felt so good, so relaxed, more relaxed than he'd felt in weeks. And he'd forgotten how comfy this old sofa was. His eyes drifted shut.

He was jarred awake by the simultaneous sounds of his phone's text ringtone and keys jangling in the door. Where was he? What was he doing in his office, what time was it?

"Hellooo, who's here already?" called Ida. "Silvio?" She walked over to the sofa and stood over him, hands on her hips. "Aw. Hon, don't tell me you spent the night here."

"What?" Silvio said groggily, "What time is it?"

Ida glanced at her watch, "It's like, six forty-five."

Silvio sat up. "Six forty-five? Holy crow!" He felt around the sofa for his phone and found it wedged between the cushions. He saw that he had a text from Charleston. If he could be at Charleston's office by seven forty-five Charleston would see him. Silvio sprang up from the sofa. "Geeze, I'll never make it!"

"Make what, Hon?"

"Ida, I'm sorry, I gotta...look, could you call my Uncle Bud, see if he can go help Kevin with that nine a.m. contract piping system out in Willow Grove? If Bud can't do it, then...see what the new kid, Shawn, is doing, otherwise I'll have to..." Silvio rubbed his hands over his face. "I'll have to..."

"Whatever you gotta do, go do it," Ida said, putting a motherly hand on his arm. "We'll manage. Go in the bathroom, throw some water on your face, brush your teeth, and I'll make you a cup of instant to grab on your way out."

"Ida, you're the best," Silvio said, his eyes threatening to tear up as he hurried toward the bathroom.

"Don't worry about it, Hon."

***

"So you're telling me, Mr. Jablonski, that Trysta now wants to end the proceedings and give you full legal and physical custody of your children?"

"Well, she wants visitation. I'll give her visitation. All she wants. I mean, the kids need their mother, too. Even if..."

"Even if what?"

"Aw, I don't know. I mean, it's crazy, but..."

"But what?"

Silvio blushed and rubbed the back of his neck. "All of a sudden Trysta thinks she's...I don't know...gay."

Charleston cocked his head and frowned as if trying to make sense of what he'd just heard. "Trysta – your ex-wife – she's...gay?"

"I mean, she *says* she is. Huh, couldn't of proved it by me. Aw, what the heck do I know? I feel like I don't know anything about anything anymore." Silvio sighed. "Anyway, Trysta says she's gay and she wants to go back to school and learn to support herself...I mean, I don't know about the gay part...but I guess it's good she wants to learn to take care of herself instead of, you know, throwing herself at men like she's done."

"I see," said Charleston. "Well, if your ex-wife is agreeable and you're agreeable and the children seem agreeable to the arrangement..."

"Oh yeah, my kids." Silvio ran a hand through his hair. "That's another thing. I talked to them last night. They seemed kind of rattled. Something about some people came over and banged at the door and the kids and Trysta got scared and Darren made them hide in the closet. Then the police came with guns looking for the bad guys but the bad guys were actually good guys, or something, and they all had to come out of the closet and put their hands up. It sounds crazy. I talked to Trysta, she laughed it off, said it was just a big mistake, wrong house, whatever, but now here I am worried about my kids, wondering what the heck is going on in that crazy rich neighborhood with the police pointing guns at my poor kids."

Charleston shook his head. "That does sound...very strange. Of course the police do raid the wrong house from time to time – though I'd imagine less often in a neighborhood such as your ex-wife's."

"Huh, not like they're a bunch of saints out in that neighborhood, either," said Silvio.

"Indeed not," Charleston chuckled.

"They just don't get caught as much."

"I would personally agree with you on that, Mr. Jablonski. Still, if what your children have told you is accurate then the episode was inexcusable and you may have grounds for legal recourse if you'd like to pursue it."

"Yeah, well, the whole thing makes me mad, and all, but no, I don't want to do any...legal recourse. I just want to get my kids out of there and back here with me. Especially since Trysta and Darren will be splitting up now that she's...gay."

"All right. Well, this being the case, I'd venture to say that we can likely bring about this outcome fairly smoothly. Do you foresee that your ex-wife will want legal representation?"

Silvio shrugged. "She didn't say anything about that. I mean, we both want the same thing, right?"

"If that is in fact the case then I could represent both of your interests and those of your children. Do you think that would be acceptable to Trysta?"

"Yeah, well, I'll ask her. Then what happens?"

"Then your case will go before a family court judge, though none of you would necessarily have to appear before the judge in person provided everyone is as agreeable as it appears. I would file the papers in your behalf. It would be a few weeks or months until the new custody arrangement was formalized in the eyes of the court, but in the meantime – again, if everyone agrees – the children could move in with you at any time."

"Any time?"

"Any time they and their mother wished."

Silvio felt at a loss for words. He blinked back tears.

Charleston continued. "Now what about the baby, Silvia? Does Trysta want to give you long-term or permanent legal guardianship of her as well?"

Silvio wiped his eyes. "Yeah, she says she does."

"In that case your legal guardianship will likewise have to be approved by the judge, but again, in view of the cordiality among you all, I can file for you."

"And I can take Silvia home with me any time, too?"

Charleston smiled. "Any time you and Trysta want."

"What the heck's wrong with me?" said Silvio, pulling a handkerchief from his pocket, "I feel like I'm gonna start crying."

Charleston said sympathetically, "Why don't you get back to Trysta and propose to her that you and she and I and whoever else she wishes to be present meet here in my office and I'll draw up the legal papers which I will then file with the judge."

"That's all we have to do?"

Charleston smiled again. "That's all."

"Wow," said Silvio, "how easy is it when we all agree?"

"An astute observation," said Charleston.

"Hey, can I bring Sally with me?"

"You may," said Charleston, "as long you're sure your ex-wife won't mind her presence. How is Mrs. Miller doing? Well, I hope."

"Sally? Oh, yeah, she's fine. She's just about always fine." Silvio smiled affectionately. "We're getting married."

"Congratulations," Charleston said warmly. "Have you set a date?"

"Nah, not yet. I've been so wrapped up in all this, with the kids and all, that I…" Silvio looked down at his hands. "I don't know, I think I might have been neglecting Sally."

Charleston's smile faded. "You've been neglecting Sally?"

"Well…yeah. Kind of. I guess I've been sort of, you know, leaving her out."

"Leaving her out?"

"Of all this. It's just been easier not to talk about it."

Charleston nodded. "You know," he said, "I'd been wondering why Mrs. Miller suddenly stopped coming to our appointments. After all, though it may be understandably difficult to discuss, the issue of your children's custody does involve her. Especially now that you're engaged, I should think."

Silvio pulled in a deep breath. "Yeah, well, it's just…I stopped asking her to come with me because…You remember how it went last time she came?"

"Yes, said Charleston, "I do remember. I remember that Mrs. Miller was upset, but frankly, it seemed to me that she made some legitimate observations and had some legitimate concerns. And, Mr. Jablonski, you must understand that at this moment she may be feeling somewhat insecure in your relationship, especially if you've been, as you admit, neglecting her and shutting her out of what you've been going through because you don't want to talk about it or hear what she has to say."

"Yeah," said Silvio, "yeah. Well, from now on it'll be different."

"Good. Because as someone who's overseen the break-up of too many couples who've fallen out of love for a variety of reasons great and small, I'm telling you: *Don't neglect Sally.*"

"Right." Silvio stood. "Okay, well, thanks, I'll call you later, I'll call Trysta, I'll…I gotta go."

After Silvio left his office Charleston shook his head. A gay ex-wife. A police raid. Now possible clouds on the horizon with Sally. No, it was never simple.

Chapter Fourteen

Angelo Barbieri's young second wife Nicole stood at her husband's desk and studied the paper that was about to become the title to her new Jaguar.

"Hurry up, Mommy," said six-year-old Abington Barbieri, pulling on her mother's sleeve, "we have to go shopping!"

"Yeah, sign the damn thing before Jason Trump here changes his mind." Angelo Barbieri cocked his head towards Geoffry, who stood next to him looking battered and miserable with a black eye and a bandage on his nose. "Whataya say, J.T.," laughed Angelo, "you having any second thoughts about selling my wife your new Jag?"

Geoffry shook his head and stifled a sob.

"Geeze, what happened to you anyway, Geoffry?" asked Nicole. "I mean with your face all banged up like that?"

"I"

"Old Geoffry here tripped in the parking lot," Angelo cut him off, "walking over to his new car, didn't you?" Angelo threw and arm over Geoffry's shoulder. "Busted his nose good. But he's okay, aren't you J.T.?" Angelo gave Geoffry's shoulder a hard squeeze. Geoffry winced. "Come one, Nic, sign it." Angelo pointed to the signed sentence Geoffry had hand-written on the back of the title turning his new car over to Nicole Barbieri. "Sign it there. I'll get my lawyer to notarize it when he gets back from Tahiti."

"Aw, I don't know, Angelo," Nicole whined, "I wanted a black XE Compact Sport , not a silver XKG. This one's tacky."

"Just *sign* it, Nicole," said Angelo. "I have to get back to fucking work."

"Just *sign* it, Mommy," cried Abington, "we have to go fucking shopping!"

"Hey, hey, hey," Laughed Angelo, lifting up his daughter, "you're not supposed to use that word. Only Daddy uses that word, not you."

Nicole rolled her eyes. "See what happens? You don't use that word Abby, you hear? People'll think you're a little *fighett.'*"

"*Oooo*okay," Abington sighed. She wriggled down from her father's arms. "Now give us some money, Daddy. We hafta go shopping."

"Just as soon as your Mommy signs."

"*Sign*, Mommy, *sign!*"

"Fine," Nicole snapped. "There. I signed."

"Now give us our money, Daddy!"

Angelo reached into his pocket for his wallet. "So how come all you ever do is go shopping, huh? What about that fancy school I'm sending you to? What kind of school is it? A shopping school?"

Abington giggled. "No, Daddy, it's *kindergarten!*"

"Kindergarten, huh? Well, how come you're not there?"

"*Teacher's* meeting, Daddy!"

Angelo shook his head. He pulled a wad of bills from his wallet and handed it to his young wife. "Here. Go shopping. Spend all my money. Now get outta here so Geoffry and me can make some more. Geoffry, pull out your phone and call that useless brother of yours. Tell him get his ass in here."

Nicole snatched the money from her husband's hand and kissed his cheek. She counted it out then held up the bills. "*Seriously*, Angelo? Two-fifty?"

"We need more, Daddy!"

"Yeah, we need more, Daddy," said Nicole.

"More? Whataya need more"

"Darren's not picking up," Geoffry interrupted, "Should I"

"Yeah, yeah, do whatever," Angelo cut him off. "*Mama mia*, this place is a freakin'"

"Mr. Barbieri?" Dina's voice came over his desk intercom.

"Dina, this place is a freakin' circus! *I pagliacci!*"

"Uh, Mr. Barbieri?" Dina said softly.

"What?"

"There are a couple of um…they look like police officers outside the door."

"Aw, get rid of 'em!"

A few moments later Dina buzzed back.

"I couldn't. They're federal agents. They're, uh, on their way up. Now here come some cops after them.

"Oh, fuck, fuck, *fuck!*"

"Angelo?" Nicole ran a hand through her long layered blond hair. "Did she say federal agents were on their way up? And cops? Oh Jesus Christ, Angelo, what did you *do?*"

"Daddy, what did you *do?*" mimicked Abington, her mother in miniature down to the fisted hand on her hip.

Ignoring his wife and daughter, Angelo yanked open the bottom desk of his drawer and rummaged around until he found a small envelope which he nervously ripped open.

"Geoffry, shut the door! *Shut the fuckin' door!*"

But Geoffry had already exited Angelo's office, leaving the door open after him.

"Oh, Christ, that *moron!*" Angelo pulled a flash drive from the envelope then hurried towards the open door to close it. "Here," he said to Nicole, handing her the flash drive on his way to the door, "go the bathroom, shut the door and flush this down the toilet, *now!*"

"Huh?" said Nicole dumbly, holding up the flash drive, "You want me to flush this down the toilet?"

Angelo was stopped at the door by Geoffry flanked by Agent Robbi Downer and Agent Miggy Corazón, each of them gripping one of Geoffry's arms.

"Miss, I wouldn't flush anything down the toilet if I were you," said Agent Downer.

The two federal agents pushed Geoffry back into Angelo's office. Four police officers entered and four more plainclothes men and women entered behind them. Nicole Barbieri, wide-eyed with fear, dropped the flash drive.

The agents let go of Geoffry then each reached into their pocket and pulled out a badge.

"Internal Revenue Service," said Miggy Corazón.

"FBI," said Robbi Downer. "Angelo Barbieri?"

Angelo stepped back without answering.

"Angelo Barbieri?" Miggy Corazón repeated, but Angelo remained silent.

"Oh, for God's sake, Angelo," cried Nicole, "What's the matter? Whyncha *answer* them?"

"*Answer* them, Daddy!" echoed Abington, grabbing her mother's hand.

"Aw, geeze, Nicole, can't you just keep your mouth shut for once?"

"Angelo Barbieri," said the IRS agent, "I have a warrant to search your business and personal records on suspicion of tax fraud and money laundering. Federal agents are also searching your home at this time. Any attempt to obstruct this search in any way is a federal offense." The agent turned to the plain clothes agents behind him. "Start with that flash drive on the floor."

"Am I in trouble?" asked Nicole Barbieri in a trembling voice.

"Not unless you've done something wrong, Hon," replied Robbi.

"Am I in trouble?" asked Abington Barbieri, her eyes filling with tears.

"Did you do anything wrong, Baby?" asked Robbi.

"*Noooo!*" wailed Abington, "I d-didn't d-do anything! I w-w-want to go *home!*"

"Well, ask your mama to take you home, then," Robbi said gently.

"Come on, Abby," said Nicole, whisking her daughter out of the office, stopping at the door just long enough to turn back to her husband and snap, "Angelo, you *asshole!*"

Under the direction of Robbi Downer the plainclothes agents ransacked the office to the protests of Barbieri, who threatened to call his lawyer, to sue, and to have their jobs, to which one of the plainclothes agents replied, "So call your lawyer, sue, and you want this fuckin' job you can have it."

Agent Downer, followed by the two police officers, walked over to Geoffry, who'd fled to a far corner of the room where he sat on the floor cowering as if trying to make himself invisible.

The agent spoke down to Geoffry while the police officers appeared to be stifling laughter. "Geoffry Steubing? You are wanted for questioning regarding tax fraud and money laundering by your employer, Angelo Bar"

"No!" Geoffry cut in, "That's not me! You got the wrong guy!"

"Geoffry Steubing," Agent Downer began again, "you are wanted for questioning regarding"

"I'm telling you, that's not me! I, I don't know who that is!"

"You're not Geoffry Steubing?" asked Agent Downer.

Geoffry, raised himself to his knees, tears in his eyes, his arms open in a gesture of supplication. "No, no! I swear, I never heard of any Geoffry Steubing! I *swear!*"

"You don't work for this guy?"

"No, no, I never, I never even been up here before!"

"You're not Geoffry Steubing? And you never even been up here before?"

"That's right! That's right!"

"Well who the hell are you then," asked Agent Downer, "and what are you doing here?"

"I'm, I'm...*Jason! Jason Trump!*"

"Jason Trump?" asked the agent.

"Any relation to Donald?" asked one of the police officers.

"Yes! No! I mean, yes! I mean no!"

"Well, what is it?" asked the other police officer, "yes or no?"

"I, I, I...I'm not the guy!"

"*Which* guy?" asked the police officer while Robbi Downer rolled her eyes, "Geoffry Steubing or Jason Trump?"

Angelo, who'd given up protesting, now sat at his desk looking crumpled and pale as he listlessly watched Geoffry's interrogation. "Aw bag it, Geoffry," he called dryly, "you'll only make it worse for yourself with these assholes."

"I'm not Geoffry Steubing!" Geoffry broke into loud breathless sobs. "I'm not...I'm not...I'm not..."

"Yeah, you are, you dumb pussy *oobatz*," sighed Angelo.

The police officers sniggered softly while Robbi Downer struggled to squelch her own laughter. Finally the agent cleared her throat and said, "Geoffry Steubing, you are now under arrest for obstruction of justice. You have the right to remain silent."

The police officers pulled Geoffry to his feet and handcuffed him while Agent Downer continued reading Geoffry his rights, after which she said to the officers, "You can take this guy away. But go easy on him. He already looks pretty banged up." Geoffry's crying could be heard in the room as the police officers walked him down the hall to the elevator.

Angelo shook his head and laughed weakly. "Excuse my language, Miss," he said to Agent Downer, "but is that guy not the dumbest fuck you ever met?"

Robbi Downer ignored Angelo's question but joined her IRS brethren who were congregated around the wall safe they'd discovered behind a large painting. "Can we have the key to this safe, please?" the FBI agent asked Angelo.

"I don't have it," Barbieri replied.

"Can you get it real fast?" Agent Downer asked, "Or do you want to join your dumb fuck friend?"

Angelo cursed under his breath but opened a drawer with a false back that the agents had missed in their search and pulled out a key. "Here," he said with bitter resignation, "knock yourself out."

From the deep, wide safe the agents removed two large valises, each filled with cash. The IRS agents began snapping photos of the cash while Miggy Corazón called for a few more back-up police officers. Then Agent Corazón turned to Angelo. "Angelo Barbieri," he said, "you are under arrest on suspicion of income tax evasion. You have the right to remain silent."

"Aw, fuck me!" muttered Angelo, hoping his lawyer was back from his vacation in Tahiti.

Chapter Fifteen

Joanne stopped by Sally's desk where Sally sat typing on her laptop, absorbed in her work.

"Yo, Sally, didja get those receivables entered? 'Cause I got a project here, Rynkowski is sending back a whole file, a real screwed-up data bitch that's gonna take the rest of the day to untangle, thanks to the great work of one of your co-workers, I won't say who."

"Screwed-up bitch who can't even figure out how to enter data?" Sally said sourly, continuing to tap on her keyboard while looking at the computer screen. "Say no more. Cammie T. strikes again." Sally stopped typing and looked up at Joanne. "Yeah, send me the Rynkowski file. I'll fix Cammie's mistakes. *Again.* Seriously, Joanne, I don't know why you're always covering her ass."

"Yeah, well, that's what I do, right? Sometimes I cover Cammie's ass," Joanne gave Sally a sharp look, "and sometimes I cover Sally's."

Sally slumped in her chair. "Aw, I'm sorry, Joanne, I guess I'm in kind of a bitchy mood myself this morning."

"Uh, *yeah*," said Joanne. "You look like you're carrying twenty pounds of sand on your shoulders."

"Yeah, well…" Sally shook her head then returned to her typing. "One of those days, I guess."

"You start your next round of classes yet?"

"A couple weeks. Accounting and Java Script, whatever the hell that is. I bought the books."

146

"Ought to keep you busy."

"Yeah," Sally said hoarsely.

Joanne hesitated then asked, "So how's Silvio?"

"Silvio," said Sally.

"Silvio," said Joanne.

Sally stopped typing. "He doesn't call, he doesn't..." She unconsciously glanced at her hand.

"Give you a ring?"

"Huh," Sally laughed humorlessly, "I've given up on thinking that'll happen. I think...I think he's ghosting me now. Trying to just...disappear."

"Aw, now, do you know that for sure?"

"I don't know anything for sure." Sally reached across her desk for her cellphone and opened the screen. "He sent me a text at seven-thirty this morning. It said, 'I got the kids, explanation point.'"

"He got the kids, explanation point?"

"I figure it must have been a butt text."

"A butt text? How do you butt text?"

"I mean like he meant to send it to somebody else. He probably meant it for, I don't know... Trysta."

"Aw, come on," said Joanne. "Look, Silvio's gonna call you. Eventually."

"Yeah. Eventually. Maybe." Sally sniffed and blinked her eyes. "It's been hard, you know?"

Joanne put a hand on Sally's shoulder. "I know, Hon."

"If Silvio wants to go it alone..."

"Aw, Sally..."

"I guess it's just as well he hasn't given me a ring, because I'm not even sure anymore I want to..." Sally rubbed a sleeve across her eyes then went back to her typing. "So yeah, send me that data file that Cammie screwed up. What's one more damn mess?"

Joanne sighed and squeezed Sally's shoulder.

***

Silvio hurried into the front office of Zarnecki and Young and approached the reception desk where a pretty young receptionist wearing a single-ear headset sat typing at her keyboard.

The young receptionist looked up and smiled. "My goodness, what beautiful flowers," she said in a soft, smooth voice, eying the bouquet of roses in the cut glass vase that Silvio carried.

"They're for Sally," Silvio said breathlessly, "Sally Miller."

"Well, I'm sure she'll love them," said the receptionist. "Special occasion?"

"No, well, yeah, well...I just wanted to bring her some flowers."

"That's nice. You just leave them here on my desk and I'll bring them right back to Sally."

"Uh, I wanted to...I mean, can I bring them back to her myself?"

"Oh...you want to bring them to her yourself?"

"Yeah."

"Just a moment, please." The receptionist tapped her keyboard then scrolled down with her mouse. "Mrs. Ponticello?" she said into her headset, "There's a gentleman out here who would like to bring some flowers back to Sally..." The receptionist looked up at Silvio and smiled. "Could I have your name please?"

"Silvio."

"His name is Silvio...all right, I'll tell him. 'Bye." To Silvio she said, still smiling, "Mrs. Ponticello will be right out." She then returned to typing on her laptop.

"Wait...Joanne Ponticello is coming out here?"

The receptionist looked up at Silvio and smiled again. "She'll be right out. Why don't you have a seat?"

"But why...?"

"You can sit right over there," said the receptionist pleasantly, pointing to two plush armchairs around a coffee table on which sat several magazines.

Silvio looked around, an uneasy feeling rising up from the pit of his stomach. The receptionist continued tapping on her keyboard. He walked over the waiting area, set the flowers on the coffee table and sat in one of the armchairs. He tapped his fingers on the arm rest.

When Joanne entered the reception area Silvio rushed over to her. "Where's Sally? Is anything wrong? Is she all right?"'

"Let's talk over here, Hon," said Joanne, leading Silvio back to the sitting area. After they'd sat down Joanne said, "Yeah, I'd say there's something wrong, and Sally's been better."

"What's wrong? Is she sick? Why didn't she tell me?" Silvio's face was a study in distress.

"She's not sick, except for her heart, and apparently she's been trying to tell you this, but…"

"I been neglecting her," Silvio said miserably.

"You've been shutting her out," Joanne said. "Look, God knows you've been going through a rough time emotionally with the custody battle and now this paternity *agita*. And I'm plenty sympathetic. But you shut Sally out when she wanted to be there for you – even though she's up to her neck with work and school and trying to care for those two little boys – and now she thinks you want to go it alone. Without her."

"No, no," Silvio cried, "I don't want to go it alone! I love her! I want to marry her!"

The receptionist looked over but darted quickly back to her laptop when Joanne caught her eye.

Joanne lowered her voice. "See, Sally's not so sure of that these days. And I hate to tell you, Silvio, but she's not so sure how *she* feels about the idea anymore, either."

Silvio reached for the vase of flowers and stood up. "I'll tell her right now, I'll"

"Give her a ring," Joanne cut him off.

Silvio looked taken aback. "A ring? Well…yeah…sure…I mean, I'm gonna give her a ring, I just…with all that's been going on…but, sure, I'm gonna get her a ring."

"Get her one now."

"You mean, like…*right* now?"

"I'll be straight with you, Silvio. I don't know how serious Sally is about wanting to bail on this relationship, but if I were you I'd…"

"I'll get her a ring! I'll get her one right now! I shoulda got her one weeks ago, what the heck's the matter with me?"

"But, Hon, it's gonna take more than a ring, you know that, right?"

"I just…I didn't know she was so upset."

"She's upset."

"I'll get her a ring!" he almost shouted.

"Get her a ring. For starters. Then quit shutting her out."

"I gotta go. Thanks, Joanne." Silvio gave Joanne a clumsy hug, still holding the vase of flowers.

"You're welcome, Silvio."

Silvio hurried towards the door of the building then turned and hurried back to Joanne. "I don't know where to go. To buy a ring."

"Where'd you buy Trysta's ring?"

Silvio looked sheepish. "Actually…my Aunt Celeste picked out the ring for me. And my Uncle Bud paid for it because I didn't have any money. I was, what, eighteen?"

Joanne smiled. "Okay, you want to go to Harry the Ring King."

"Oh yeah, I think that's where my Aunt Celeste picked out Trysta's ring."

"Probably. Everybody goes to Harry's. It's not far from here, out on Rising Sun Avenue."

"Oh, yeah, I know where Rising Sun is."

"It's at Rising Sun and Magee."

"Yeah, sure, I know Rising Sun and Magee. I'm going. Right now." Silvio hurried away again then turned back again to Joanne. "Thanks again, Joanne."

"You're welcome. And don't spend too much, okay?"

"Okay," Silvio called back on his way out the door. Then he stopped again. "What size do you think Sally is? In a ring, I mean?"

Joanne stood open-mouthed.

"Probably a size six, like me," called the receptionist. Then she added, sheepishly, "Sorry. The acoustics here are really good."

Joanne sighed as Silvio hurried out the door. "I hope this works," she said softly.

Chapter Sixteen

"What, you came in?" Ellie Krillman called to Darren as he walked by the open door of her office.

"Yeah, I thought I might as well." *After those two cops last night told me to,* he said to himself.

"Yeah, you might as well," said Ellie. *You might as well be here for the shit show, too,* she said to herself. She knew that her call to the FBI last night after Jeremy Andrews ordered her to fire Darren was the right thing to do, still she was dreading the *Gotterdammerung* that was about to come sweeping through the prestigious door of Highland and Erskerberg. Ellie took a sip of the hot water with lemon on her desk. She was too nervous for coffee this morning.

Half an hour later Darren heard a rustle of activity and looked up to see agents Robbi Downer and Miggy Corazón followed by a cadre of police officers tromping through the main floor then into the elevator that led to the executive offices. After the elevator doors shut Ellie Krillman stepped from her office onto the floor and shot around a look that said, *You saw nothing. Get back to work.* Everyone turned back to their work until the elevator doors slid open again and Jeremy Andrews stepped out flanked by the police officers, his hands cuffed and his arms gripped by two of the officers. There were gasps, stares, and whispers, but after the parade exited the office Ellie Krillman was again out on the floor with her silent discreet warning and everyone again returned to their work.

Darren's heart was pounding in his chest. He'd been half expecting to be grabbed and cuffed himself. He heaved a great sigh of relief.

***

"Oh, you're back," said the smiling, silken-voiced receptionist as Silvio once again breathlessly approached her desk. He still carried the vase of roses in one arm, but now he held in the other a small white bag on which was written in effusive gold lettering, "Harry the Ring King." The receptionist leaned towards Silvio and said even more softly, "Did you get the ring?"

"Yeah," said Silvio, blushing. He held up the bag.

"Just a second," said the receptionist, tapping and scrolling. "Mrs. Ponticello?" she said into her headset, "Silvio's back." She lowered her voice conspiratorially, sounding delighted. "He's got the ring....Oh…" Her smile faded. She looked up at Silvio. "Mrs. Ponticello says you don't want to give it to her here in the office."

"I want to give it to her right now! I don't wanna wait another second!"

"He wants to give it to her right now. He doesn't want to wait another second...Okay, I'll tell him. She says you want to give it to her someplace nice."

Silvio spread his arm towards the chairs in the waiting area. "It's nice right here."

"He says it's nice right here in the lobby…" The receptionist looked at Silvio. "Mrs. Ponticello says the lobby is a, um, bleeping fish bowl."

"Tell her I'm gonna have to work late tonight then I gotta get my kids. And from then on my life is gonna be crazy."

"He says he has to work late tonight and then get his kids and then…" The receptionist's face lit up. "Okay, I'll tell him. 'Bye." The receptionist said to Silvio, "Mrs. Ponticello is sending Sally right out."

"Yeah, well, Joanne thinks I'm crazy."

The receptionist again leaned towards Silvio. "I think it's sweet." She gestured towards the chairs. "Go wait over there. Surprise her!"

Sally entered the lobby and walked over to the receptionist's desk. "What's up, Sarah? Joanne told me to"

"Over there," the receptionist interrupted her, pointing towards Silvio, who had moved the chairs and table behind a pillar, out of eye and ear shot of the receptionist's desk.

Silvio hurried towards Sally, who instinctively hurried towards him and hugged him. "What's going on?"

Silvio held her close for a moment then kissed her forehead. "I have so much to tell you. But first...come over here." He led her to the chairs and the coffee table on which sat the vase of roses and the Harry the Ring King bag. "Sit," he said, then he pulled a small blue velvet box from the bag and got down on one knee before Sally.

"Wait," said Sally, putting her hand over his to prevent him from opening the box, "wait. Tell me first what you have to tell me. Because you sure haven't been telling me much lately." Sally's eyes filled with tears.

"Aw, Sally, Sally, don't cry," Silvio said gently. He reached into his pocket for his handkerchief.

"Oh, don't worry about it," said Sally, taking his handkerchief, "just...just...*talk*."

"Sally, I got the kids."

Sally's eyes widened, "You got the kids? *Your* kids? You got your kids?"

"I got my kids, Sally. Trysta gave me my kids. Full custody. No more courts, no more fighting. Sally, I got my kids!" Silvio, still on his knees, lowered his head and sobbed into Sally's lap.

"Oh my God Silvio," Sally said softly, stroking his head, "that's wonderful." She lifted his head and kissed him. "That's wonderful. Wait a minute." She stood then stepped over to the other chair and pulled it across from hers. "Here, sit down. Tell me everything."

Silvio sat in the chair, set the ring box on the floor and took Sally's hands in his. "She called me last night while I was in my office. Well, the kids called me first, then...Aw, Sally, I was gonna call you right away, all I wanted to do was call you and tell you, but it was eight o'clock, I knew you'd be putting the boys down so I figured I'd wait ten minutes. I laid down on the sofa, just for ten minutes, see, and next thing I know Ida is waking me up."

Sally laughed and squeezed his hand. "I believe you Silvio. You've been so tired lately, with all this going on."

"I've been so tired." Silvio lowered his head and began sobbing again. "Sally I've been *so tired.*"

"I know, Baby, I know." Sally leaned towards him and wiped his eyes then rubbed his shoulders.

Silvio looked up into Sally's eyes. "And I know I haven't been good to you lately, either. I'm so sorry, Sally. I been going a little crazy since this whole thing with Silvia started. I'm sorry, Sally, I'm so sorry."

"I know, I know, it's okay. But what about Silvia now?"

"Trysta's gonna give me guardianship of Silvia, too. Permanent legal guardianship."

"Wow," said Sally.

"I ran over to see Charleston first thing this morning. That's why I only had time to text you real quick, I slept so late and all."

"Wait, was that the text that said, 'I got the kids?'"

"Yeah, you got it? I thought maybe you didn't get it."

"Well, yeah I got it, but…oh, never mind, so what did Charleston say to you?"

"He said that if Trysta wants me to take all the kids, even Silvia, then it shouldn't be any problem. We'll just have to all have a meeting with Charleston and he'll file some paperwork with the judge. But I can basically have the kids anytime. Have them come back and live with me, even."

"Silvio, that's so great. But what happened? With Trysta, I mean? Why did she all of a sudden change her mind? And she's even giving you Silvia?"

Silvio chuckled and shook his head. "This you're really not gonna believe. Trysta…I guess she's been seeing a psychologist."

"What?" Sally laughed.

"Yeah. Zach's psychologist, Dr. Cavanni. Trysta's been seeing her. For herself."

"About time Trysta started seeing a psychologist," Sally chuckled.

"Yeah," Silvio chuckled. "Anyway, now here's what you're not gonna believe, Trysta has figured out that she's…gay."

"*What?*"

The receptionist, jarred by the sudden whoop of laughter that carried over to her desk, stood and tried to crane her neck to see around the pillar. Disappointed, she sat back down and returned to her laptop.

"Trysta's *gay?*" Sally laughed. "With all those *guys?* You're kidding me, right?"

"Yeah, that's what I thought at first, too. But now…I don't know, the more I think about it the more I can kind of…" Silvio shrugged.

"…see it," Sally finished Silvio's sentence. "Yeah, I guess that might make some sense. Why she is the way she is. Why she can do so much sex with so many men without any real…" Sally shrugged, too.

"Yeah, without any real…"

"Yeah."

Silvio and Sally burst out laughing.

"Hey, it's not like any of this is actually funny," said Sally, wiping her eyes.

"No it's not," said Silvio, suddenly serious, "but that's how it is. And if you won't forgive me and you won't marry me, then I don't know what I'm gonna"

Sally covered his lips with her fingertips. "I do and I will. But only on one condition."

"What," said Silvio, his eyes wide with dismay.

"You've got to forgive me, too. For being too emotional sometimes. For not always being quiet and just listening when that's what you needed me to do. For maybe even being a little…jealous through all this."

"Jealous?"

"Yeah. And I apologize for it. And I love you."

"Aw, Baby." Silvio stood and lifted Sally to her feet then took her into his arms and held her close. "I love you so much. So much." He pulled away from her. "Okay, now sit down again." After she was seated he got back down on one knee and picked up the ring box from the floor beside him and opened the box, proffering the ring to Sally. "Sally, will you still marry me?"

Sally gazed at the white-gold ring set with a delicate princess-cut diamond then looked up at Silvio. "What, no cake?" Then she laughed and hugged Silvio. "Yes, yes, yes!"

Silvio slipped the ring onto Sally's finger. The size six was a perfect fit. "I promise you, Sally, you'll have it all. Our kids, a big house, money, your law degree...someday."

"In the meantime I'll settle for you. And all our kids, of course."

"Let's get married right away," said Silvio, "can we do that? Get married, and then have the honeymoon and the new house and all the other stuff later?"

"Sure," Sally chuckled. "If we can ever find the time to get married."

"Yeah," Silvio sighed. He stood up. "I should really get back to work."

"Me, too," said Sally, also standing. "I don't want to test Joanne's patience any more than I have to."

"Here, these are for you, too," said Silvio, handing Sally the vase of roses. "Put 'em on your desk." He gave her a quick kiss. "Now get back to work while I put this furniture back."

The receptionist broke into a smile as she saw Sally approach, the vase of roses in her arm and the ring sparkling on her finger. "Sally, let me see," she said, standing and reaching for Sally's hand. "Oh, it's beautiful. And a perfect fit." She came around in front of her desk to give Sally a hug. "I'm so happy for you. You've got to show Joanne. She'll be over the moon for you."

Sally laughed. "Believe me, Sarah, I'm heading straight to Joanne's office. These flowers ought to be for her."

"What? Flowers for me?" Joanne stepped into the lobby. "Oh, my God, Girl, is that what I think it is on your third finger left hand?" Sally set her flowers on the receptionist's desk and held out her hand. "Oh, my God, it's gorgeous," Joanne cried, then she hugged Sally, rocking her in her arms. "The boy did good," said Joanne, tears running down her cheeks.

"He did, Joanne," said Sally, rubbing her eyes with her sleeve.

"Here," said Sarah the receptionist, offering the women a box of Kleenex, of which she had already availed herself to wipe her own eyes.

Silvio was carrying the last chair back to its assigned spot. "Hey, what's all this crying?" he said.

"Congratulations, Silvio," called Sarah.

"Get on over here, Mister," called Joanne, her arms opened to him as he walked over to the group. "Congratulations, Hon," she said as they hugged, "You don't know how happy I am."

"I know how happy *I* am," said Silvio. "Thanks, Joanne. I don't know how I'll every thank you for"

"Oh, quit," Joanne cut him off. "So, you set a date?"

"Oh, right," laughed Sally. "We don't even know how we're gonna find the time for a wedding, crazy as things are gonna be from here on."

"We wish we could get married right now," said Silvio, putting an arm around Sally's shoulder.

"Yeah," Sally sighed. "If only we could snap our fingers and be married right here."

"Actually, you could," said Sarah the receptionist.

"Could what?" said Joanne.

"Could get married. Right here. Right now." Sarah laughed at the bewildered looks on the faces of Sally, Silvio and Joanne. "I'm a minister," she explained.

"*You* are?" said Sally, still confused.

"See, my cousin wanted to marry a Jain boy, and"

"A Jane boy?" said Joanne. "You mean like he was, what, *gay?*"

"*No,*" Sarah laughed. "Jain is an Indian religion. Jindatt is from India. And my cousin's parents, being strict Catholics, weren't having it."

"His family have money?"

"Well, that was another thing. Jindatt's family isn't rich, or anything. If they were rich I'm sure it would have been different, you know what I mean?"

"Oh, yeah," said Joanne. "I know what you mean by that. Money can wash away a lot of sins, right?"

"Only Jindatt's family doesn't really have any. They just own a vegetarian restaurant over in Mayfair. You should actually try it some time, it's over on Frankfort Avenue, not that far from here and the food's really good. It's called 'Dharma.' Anyway, Jindatt's parents are really strict Jainists and were also totally against them getting married. So my sister and I and my cousin's sister and Jindatt's sister all got together and we planned the whole wedding. And I said the ceremony."

"Well, good for you and your sister and your cousins, and all," said Sally. "But if you're a minister how come you're working here and not in a church?"

Sarah laughed again. "I'm not a minister like that. See, I got my...ordination, or whatever...from one of those online ministries." Sarah reached under her desk, turned a combination lock, opened a drawer and reached for her purse, from which she pulled out a laminated license on which was written the words, "National Friendship Church," and below that, "Reverend Sarah O'Connor."

"And you can do weddings with this?" asked Sally.

"Weddings, baptisms, funerals, anything a real minister can do. All I had to do was sign a form promising to be a spiritual, helpful person and pay $175 for a life-time membership."

"No kidding," said Sally in wonderment, studying the card.

"But wait," said Silvio, "you said you could marry us right here? Right now?"

"Well, all you'd have to do is zip down to City Hall and get yourselves a marriage license. It's what, maybe about eleven-thirty right now? On a Friday? The Marriage Bureau shouldn't be too crowded right now. Come back here with the marriage license and I'll marry you," Sarah said cheerily. "In fact all we really have to do is fill in and sign the license and presto, you'll be married."

"That's all?" asked Silvio.

"Well, then I'd tear off my part of the license and mail it in to the State of Pennsylvania, and in a couple of weeks they'll send you back a nice certificate that you can frame, or whatever, but yes, that's basically it."

"Wow," said Sally. "That would be, like, amazing, unbelievable. But...I mean, I'm at work right now, and all." she looked at Joanne.

"Yep, you are," said Joanne. "This is a place of business, believe it or not."

As if on cue Sarah turned back to her laptop and deftly tapped a few keys. "Good morning, Zarnecki and Young, this is Sarah, how may I direct your call?" she said into her headset. "Yes, hello, Mr. Rynkowski. It just so happens that Mrs. Ponticello is right here." Sarah tapped a few more keys then handed a telephone receiver to Joanne.

Joanne raised her eyes at Sally then took the receiver. "Good morning, Mr. Rynkowski…"

"Well, that's too bad," said Silvio. "I mean that we couldn't just get married right now."

"Yeah, no fuss, no stress, just doing it," said Sally. "But I could never ask Joanne to give me a couple hours off. Not with all the slack she's always cutting me as it is. And besides, today I'm supposed to be working on this big important project that somebody else screwed up. In fact it's for Mr. Rynkowski, the guy Joanne's talking to right now."

"So Sally," said Joanne, handing the receiver back to Sarah, "I hear you haven't even started on the Rynkowski file."

"But Joanne, I couldn't, see, nobody's sent it to me yet, I swear, I've been twiddling my thumbs the whole morning waiting for that file."

Joanne laughed. "I know, I know, calm down, I'm just messing with you. Mr. Rynkowski's people dropped the ball so they won't have it to you until at least Monday afternoon, which is technically no skin off our teeth, right?"

"Right, I guess. Except now you'll have to give me something else to do for the rest of the day."

"I already got something else for you to do. You take this guy and go down to City Hall and get a marriage license. Then come back here and see Sarah."

Sally and Silvio looked at each other, momentarily drop-jawed, then they both cried out with joy and fell into each other's arms.

"You'll need a witness," said Sarah, smiling.

Sarah, Sally, and Silvio looked at Joanne, who raised her hand, pointing her index finger. "Right here."

***

As Sarah had predicted, the Philadelphia City Hall Marriage Bureau wasn't crowded – generally by early Friday afternoon everyone who was going to be married that weekend had already procured their license – and Sally and Silvio were back at the reception desk of Zarnecki and Young within an hour and a half.

"Hey, you're back," said Sarah, beaming. "Got it?"

"Right here," said Silvio, handing her the envelope holding the marriage license.

"Great. Let me just call Joanne."

"I'm psychic and I'm here," said Joanne, stepping into the lobby.

"Okay, so Sally and Silvio, you fill out and sign this part right here," said Sarah, unfolding the paper, "and then, Joanne, you sign here where it says 'witness' – oh, wait, sorry. Just go ahead and fill it all out." Sarah pressed a key on her laptop. "Good afternoon, Zarnecki and Young, this is Sarah, how may I direct your call?"

After she hung up Sarah sighed. "I'm sorry, guys, I've had a run of calls the past hour. Everybody wanting to take care of last-minute Friday afternoon stuff. Maybe we better make it quick?"

"We'll make it quick," said Sally.

"The quicker the better, you ask me," said Silvio, taking Sally's hand in his.

"Me too," said Joanne.

"Okay, then," said Sarah, "Sally and Silvio, do you…oh, snap. 'Good afternoon, Zarnecki and Young…'"

"All right, so do you?" said Joanne.

"We do," said Sally and Silvio.

Joanne cocked her head towards Sarah. "Okay, since Reverend Sarah is still on the phone, I'm gonna go ahead and pronounce you"

"Wait a minute," cried Silvio, "the rings! We don't have any wedding rings!"

"Oh, it's okay," said Sally. "I mean, I already got one ring today. That'll be good enough for now."

"Yeah, I'm sure he's good for it, aren't you Silvio?" said Joanne.

"Sure, I can run back to Harry's tomorrow and get us a couple of wedding rings."

"Okay now," said Sarah, who'd finished the call, "sorry about that. Where were we?"

"I was just about to pronounce them man and wife but now you're off the phone, you can go ahead and do it."

"By the power invested in me by the State of Pennsylvania, I now pronounce you…*Ugh!* 'Good afternoon, Zarnecki and Young…'"

"…man and wife," said Joanne. There, it's done. You're married."

Sally and Silvio whooped with joy and kissed, Silvio lifting Sally off her feet. Sarah looked up from her phone call, smiled and gave a thumbs up. Joanne hugged and kissed first Sally then Silvio, the tears again running down her cheeks, and as soon as Sarah finished her phone call she hurried around her desk and hugged the bride and groom.

"Ah, boy," said Joanne, grabbing another tissue from Sarah's desk, "that was the best wedding ever."

"Well, it was probably the shortest wedding ever," said Sarah. "But it still counts."

"Aw, thanks, Sarah," said Sally.

"And what do we owe you for marrying us?"

"My treat," said Sarah.

"How about you at least keep the roses?" said Sally, nodding towards the vase of roses she'd set on Sarah's desk earlier.

"Sure," said Sarah, "thanks."

"And now, kids, we all gotta get back to work," said Joanne.

"Right," said Sarah, returning to her spot behind her desk.

"Right," Sally sighed. She noticed that Silvio looked as sad as she suddenly felt. The last thing in the world she felt like doing was leaving Silvio and going back to work. "Right," she said, and tried to disengage herself from Silvio's arms.

But Silvio still held onto her. "The way I'm feeling I sure don't know how I'm supposed go back and spend the afternoon cleaning out an industrial sewer pipe. I'd rather be, you know, celebrating, dancing. Eating. I'm starved. Hey, we skipped lunch, didn't we?"

"I was too excited to think about it," said Sally.

"Me, too," said Silvio. "Until now."

"Tell you what," said Joanne, "I need you to let go of Sally so she can get back to work."

"Yeah, okay," said Silvio. He reluctantly unwrapped his arms from around Sally's waist.

"But why don't you follow her back to her desk and she can share her...what did you pack for lunch today, Sally?"

"Peanut butter and jelly," said Sally.

"Yeah, well, you can give half to Silvio before he leaves and eat the other half at your desk. While you're working."

"Nah, I'm not taking Sally's lunch," said Silvio. "I'll pick up something on my way to the sewer pipe."

"Aw, I'm sure she'll give you a bite or two. To hold you over."

"Of course I'll share my sandwich. Or you can at least have my bag of chips."

"Nah, I'm not gonna eat your chips or your sandwich. You need to eat it all. So you don't get hungry later."

"You're the last of the gentlemen, Silvio," said Joanne. "Okay, so you won't eat your lady's lunch, why don't you at least walk her back to her desk?"

Sally's face lit up and she grabbed Silvio's hand. "Yeah, at least walk me back to my desk."

Silvio gave Sally a one more quick kiss. "Sure. Let's go."

As soon as they stepped into the office the whole Highland and Erskerberg staff sprung up from their desks and began cheering. Sally and Silvio stopped short, wide-eyed and drop-jawed in astonishment. In the middle of the room was a long table set with deli sandwiches, soft drinks, and two sheet cakes, with "Sally" written on one and "Silvio" on the other. From the ceiling hung dozens of silver and white helium balloons, and someone had twisted white crepe paper streamers hung with crepe paper wedding bells across the room dividers.

"What the heck?" Silvio laughed.

"Joanne, what...? Who..?" Sally laughed.

"Thank Mr. Zarnecki," Joanne gestured towards the owner of Zarnecki and Young, who stood off to one side of the room, smiling, "who not only gave his permission to have the wedding reception in the office but paid for the food and decorations."

"Oh, my goodness...I...thank you, Mr. Zarnecki," said Sally, still slightly dazed.

"Wow, my head's spinning," said Silvio. "Thank you...thank you."

Mr. Zarnecki nodded and waved. "Mazel Tov, Sally and Silvio."

"And don't forget your co-workers, who hauled butt quick to get all the food and the decorations together."

"Thank you," said Sally. "You guys...you're, you're...I mean...you're all the best!"

"No, you are, Sally!" someone called.

"*Mama?*" cried Silvio as he caught sight of his mother stepping from behind a room divider and hurrying across the room towards him. He opened his arms and caught her in a tight hug.

"*Mom?*" Sally cried, opening her arms to her mother, who also stepped from behind the divider. "Oh, Mom, I'm so glad you're here!" she cried, hugging her mother tightly.

"Hey," said Joanne, "you didn't think I was gonna let you get married without telling your mothers, did you? I called Quick and Reliable Plumbers to get Silvio's mom's number, and of course Sally, your mom's is on my speed dial."

"Oh, Joanne, you're too much," said Sally, wiping her tears with her sleeve. "Mom, I'm sorry we didn't get married in church like you'd want, but"

"Never mind, Dear," her mother sniffed, wiping her eyes, "Joanne explained it to me. We'll just make sure Father Tim blesses the marriage as soon as possible."

"Yeah," said Silvio's mother, wiping her own tears, "and you're gonna have to haul over to St. Cecilia's so Father Petrocelli can give you a blessing, too." She gave him a pat on the cheek. "What's the matter you get married and you don't even tell your mother?"

"Mama, don't be mad at me when I'm so happy," said Silvio, taking Sally's hand.

"How am I supposed to be mad at you when you're so happy?" She turned to Sally. "C'mere and gimme a hug. I'm glad my son finally found you."

As Silvio's mother hugged Sally, Sally's mother turned to Silvio and hugged him. "And I'm glad Sally finally found you," she said.

"And you're all coming over on the weekend for dinner," said Silvio's mother, "so Silvio's father can yell at him for getting married all of a sudden in the middle of a Friday afternoon." She turned to her son. "You think your father can take off from the Post Office in the middle of a Friday afternoon like you millionaire businessmen?"

"Aw, Mama," Silvio laughed.

"Dinner sounds lovely," said Sally's mother, "and I'll bring dessert."

Silvio gestured to the table of food. "Hey speaking of food, my stomach's rumbling. Can we eat now?"

***

After the sandwiches were eaten, the cakes cut, several soft drink and coffee toasts made in honor of the bride and groom, and many cell phone photos snapped, one of Mr. Zarnecki standing between Sally and Silvio, an arm around the shoulder of each one, there came an announcement over the office intercom: "Sally and Silvio will now dance their first dance as Mr. and Mrs....Hey, what's your last name, Silvio?"

Silvio looked around the room and called out, "Jablonski."

"Jab...?" said the loudspeaker.

"Jablonski," Silvio repeated. "It's Polish."

"Jablo...as man and wife!"

The room burst into laughter, and as Elton's John's "Your Song" began playing over the loudspeaker Sally's co-workers herded Sally and Silvio to the middle of the room and they began dancing as the others watched, some snapping more photos.

"I guess we'll even have wedding pictures," said Sally to Silvio as they danced.

"Yeah," chuckled Silvio. "Hey, you know want I'm thinking?"

"No, what?"

"This isn't just our first dance as a married couple. It's our first dance ever."

"Oh, wow, you're right. We never danced before."

"I like it," said Silvio.

"Me, too," said Sally.

"This is the best wedding ever."

"Mmmm," Sally agreed.

Silvio pulled Sally close to him and whispered into her ear, "So if this is our wedding day, you know what that makes tonight, right?"

"Yeah..."

"Your place or mine?"

Sally laughed. "Well, mine, of course. Unless you want me to bring David and Josh along for a sleep-over."

"I can spend the night, then?"

164

"You can spend every night. For the rest of your life."

Silvio pulled her closer. "Shall I be sure and bring home some left-over cake? You know, for...*tonight?*"

Sally grinned widely. *"Yeah."*

Chapter Seventeen

Sally, Silvio and Darren sat in Charleston's office in awkward silence. Charleston stood looking out his office window at the view of Logan Square.

Charleston checked his watch then turned to the others. "Trysta knows our meeting was for eleven-thirty?"

"Yeah," said Darren, "she knows it's eleven-thirty. I reminded her last night when she stopped over."

"Trysta stopped over?" asked Silvio, "To your house?"

"Yeah. To get a couple of blankets. She says the old lady she's renting her room from skimps on the heat. And the hot water."

"Sounds like Trysta's learning about life in the real world," said Sally.

"Yep," said Darren. "Started her college classes, got a job in the computer lab, moved out of the house. She's been gone six weeks already."

"Boy," said Silvio, "who'd of thought Trysta would end up working in a college computer lab?"

"Among other things who'd of thought about Trysta," added Sally.

"Huh, tell me about *that*," said Silvio, shaking his head.

"You and me both," said Darren. He hesitated a moment then said, "So how are the kids doing?"

"They're good," said Silvio. "They like being back at their old school with their old friends. And between me and my folks and Trysta's folks and Sally coming over a lot with Josh and David, they're getting plenty of attention."

"And love," added Sally.

That conversation having run its course, the group fell back into silence. After a few moments Sally glanced at Silvio then cocked her head ever so slightly towards Darren. Silvio raised his eyebrows and ever so slightly shrugged. "Okay," she said under her breath. She cleared her throat then to Darren she said, "So how's it going with selling your house? Any nibbles yet?"

"Oh yeah, it's crazy," said Darren. "You wouldn't even believe how crazy the market's gone, now all of a sudden there's a housing shortage, even out in New Conshohocken. After Trysta and the kids left I took a couple of weeks to get the place cleaned up and sorted out, then a week and a half ago I put it on the market and already I got a contract on it. It's crazy. I mean, it's great, but it's crazy."

"Wow," said Sally.

"Well, it is a pretty nice house," said Silvio. "And New Conshohocken is a pretty nice place to live."

"Yeah," said Darren. To himself he said, *That house is a shoddy, over-sized, over-priced piece of prefabricated crap like everything else in fucking New Conshohocken and I still can't believe I actually unloaded it.*

Sally and Silvio exchanged another glance. Silvio nodded and Sally said. "Silvio and me, we found a house we like."

"You found a house?" said Darren.

"A big old house in Cornwells Heights," said Silvio.

"That's great," said Darren.

"Yeah," said Silvio. "Talk about crazy, how crazy is it us being married almost two months now and still living in separate houses? But it took us that long to find a place we liked."

"And big enough for us all," added Sally. "But it is crazy, I guess."

"Oh, trust me," interjected Charleston, "I've seen all kinds of domestic arrangements and yours is not by any stretch the most unusual one. I've had several clients who live here in the Philadelphia area whose spouses worked out of town – New York, D.C. – and commuted home on the weekends."

"Oh yeah?" said Silvio. "I'm surprised they didn't all end up divorced."

Charleston turned back towards the window for a moment then he said, "Actually, they all did."

Sally and Silvio looked at each other in dismay.

"Don't worry," Charleston laughed, "every one of those couples had far wider and more troublesome gulfs between them than physical distance."

"Phew," said Silvio, taking Sally's hand.

"But tell us about this house," said Charleston.

"Well," said Silvio, "it's a fixer-upper, but the price is right and we got time." He smiled at Sally, who smiled back at him. "And like I was just saying, my parents live there, and Trysta's parents, too. In Cornwells Heights, I mean."

"And it's close to Northeast Philly, so we're not too far from my mom, either," said Sally.

"So lots of help with the baby-sitting," Charleston chuckled.

"Yeah, that's what we're thinking," said Silvio. "Lots of support, you know?"

"We're gonna need it," said Sally, "especially with me about to start my classes again."

"Six children? A new fixer-upper house? A full-time job? *And* going back to school? I salute you, Mrs.Jablonski. And Mr. Jablonski, too. I salute you both."

"We can do it," said Silvio.

"If anyone can do it, you two can," said Charleston. "This I believe one hundred percent."

"Thanks," said Silvio.

"Except that as soon as we get into the new house I'm..." Here Sally blushed and looked at Silvio again, who nodded. "I'm quitting my job at Zarnecki and Young and I'm going to be a full-time stay-at-home mom. While I go to school."

"What?" said Darren, "You are?"

"Yeah," Sally chuckled self-consciously. "I've been working since high school. I feel like won't know how to not work."

"Oh, you'll be working plenty," said Silvio.

"Indeed you will," said Charleston.

"But see," said Sally, turning to Darren, "the thing is…" She glanced at Silvio again. "We need a real estate agent."

"You need…a real estate agent?"

"Well, yeah," said Silvio, "to sell our houses for us."

"So we can buy the new one," said Sally. "And…"

"…we wanted to ask you," Silvio finished for her.

"*Me?*" asked Darren, dumbfounded. "You want *me* to sell your houses for you?"

"Is that a problem?" asked Silvio. "'Cause if it is we can always"

"No," Darren cut him off, "no, I…I mean, that's…what I do, right? Sell houses." To himself he added, *Only I can't fucking believe you're asking me to sell yours.*

As if reading his mind Sally said, "I know we have some…history…some anger between us."

"Yeah. A little, I guess."

"Huh," Silvio grunted.

Sally patted Silvio's hand then continued, "But, whatever, we know you're a good real estate agent."

"Seeing as you work with a big downtown real estate agency, and all," added Silvio.

"But you know the Northeast, too," said Sally. "And then we figure if we pay you to sell our houses at least some of it will come back to Josh in child support, so…"

"Yeah, okay," Darren said, "I'll do it." *Their houses are cheap*, he thought, *but I need all the pocket change I can get.*

"You figure they'll sell pretty quick?" asked Silvio.

"Oh yeah, I'll have them on and off the market for you in no time."

"Speaking of time," said Charleston, glancing at his watch again.

At that moment there was a knock on the door and Charleston's assistant Maria entered from the waiting room followed by Trysta. Her formerly long blond hair had been shorn, cropped up the sides but left long at the top with layered bangs that fell almost to her eyes. She wore a long olive drab green hooded jacket over a loose, stretched-out tan sweater and baggy camouflage pants tucked into scuffed Doc Marten boots. The whole ensemble appeared to have come from a thrift store.

While everyone else stared in drop-jawed silence only Charleston seemed unruffled. He held out his hand to Trysta. "Ms. Miller? How do you do, I'm Charleston Tilley."

"I go by Trysta Wells now."

"Oh?" said Charleston. He glanced at the papers on his desk. "You've...changed your name?"

"Not yet, but I'm going to when the divorce is final."

"Should be any day now." Darren chuckled awkwardly.

"I see," said Charleston. "Well, as we're all here, shall we"

"*Dr. Cavanni?*" cried Silvio and Darren as Laura Cavanni stepped into the room behind Trysta.

"This is Doctor Laura Cavanni," said Trysta, "my, um..."

"I'm Trysta's advocate," said Dr. Cavanni with a smile. "We apologize. Trysta was detained."

"That's right," said Trysta coolly, running a hand through her cropped hair, "I was detained."

Charleston offered his hand to Laura. "Pleasure to meet you, Dr. Cavanni." He gestured towards an empty chair. "I'm sorry, I wasn't planning on an extra person. Give me a minute, I'll bring in another chair from the waiting room."

"No need, I'll stand," said Dr. Cavanni, directing Trysta to sit, then positioning herself next to Trysta's chair.

Silvio stood. "Here, take my seat."

"Oh, no thank you, Mr. Jablonski," said Dr. Cavanni, "I prefer to stand right here."

"In any case," said Charleston, "this hopefully shouldn't take too long." He took his seat at his desk and Maria sat nearby, her notebook computer poised on her lap. "Does everyone know each other, then?" Charleston asked, aware, after his years in domestic litigation, of the metaphysical rarity of people actually knowing each other.

Dr. Cavanni said, "I guess I know everyone except..." She smiled at Sally. "I expect you must be Mrs. Jablonski?"

"Huh?" said Sally, her eyes still locked on Trysta. "Oh, yeah. Hi."

"Now," said Charleston, "if I could have everyone's attention? *Please?*"

Darren and Silvio shifted their attention away from Trysta and back to Charleston, who continued, "I have here the consent forms for transference of full legal custody of Zachary, Trina and Samantha Jablonski from their mother, Trysta Miller – soon to be Wells – to their father, Silvio Jablonski, and granting of legal guardianship for Silvia Miri Miller from her parents, Darren and Trysta Miller..." He looked at Trysta, "...Ms. Wells," then he continued, "to Sally and Silvio Jablonski. Please take a moment to read over these forms."

Charleston handed out copies of the papers and waited a few minutes while everyone read them. Then he said, "Are there any questions?"

"Can I see my babies whenever I want?"

"Whenever you want to," Silvio said gently. "You just gotta let us know when you're coming."

"I want to," said Trysta. She looked down at her hands, which were folded in her lap. "It's just that..." she began twisting her fingers around each other, "I want my children to know who I am. I want them to know me as me. And there are still some things that have to happen...before I can be me."

"Yeah, sure, that's fine," said Silvio. "Go ahead and figure it all out. In the meantime our kids are in good hands. The best hands."

"Does that make me a horrible mother?"

"Trysta," said Dr. Cavanni, "don't. He told you your children are in the best hands. What better thing can a mother do for her children than to make sure they're in the best hands?"

"How are they?" Trysta asked.

"They're doing fine," said Silvio. "You don't have to worry about them."

"Do they miss me?"

"Trysta," said Dr. Cavanni, putting a hand on Trysta's shoulder.

"Hey, you come see them when you're ready, they'll be happy to see you," said Silvio.

"What about Miri?"

"My mom watches her a couple of days, your mom watches her a couple of days, Sally's mom comes over, the kids play with her, Sally and her kids come over and play with her." Silvio chuckled, "She gets passed around like a little football and she's happy as can be."

"Okay," said Trysta. She reached up and Dr. Cavanni took her hand and held it, but only for a moment.

Charleston passed pens around and after the papers were signed Trysta rubbed a hand across her eyes. She looked up at Laura and said, "I know I'm not supposed to be crying."

Laura lightly squeezed Trysta's shoulder. "It's okay just this once."

"So I guess now everything will stay the same?" said Silvio. "The kids live with me. Pretty soon Sally and me."

"Everything will stay the same," said Trysta. "But there's one more thing…" She looked up at Laura, who nodded. "…One more thing I have to tell you, Silvio. I wasn't going to, but…I have to."

Charleston squeezed his eyes shut. Not another revelation. Not another strange-but-true twist to this strange-but-true case. Not, he hoped, what he just knew he was about to hear.

"What do you wanna tell me?" said Silvio. He looked at Trysta. Her face was still beautiful and seductive despite her shorn hair, somehow more vulnerable because of it, her wide eyes full of tears, those eyes that for so many years had melted his heart, melted his will, made him feel strong and protective and weak and defenseless at the same time. That face, those eyes, Trysta's weapons for self-preservation as well as for capturing her prey. And he, too, knew.

Silvio stood. "Let me guess," he snapped. "Which one of my kids are you going to tell me isn't mine? That's what you wanna tell me, isn't it?"

Trysta sniffled. "I didn't want to tell you."

Silvio's face darkened. "Which one? Zach? Trina? Sam? All of them?"

Trysta, eyes cast downward, nodded. "Not all of them. Just"

"Stop," Silvio shouted. "I don't want to hear it."

The room went silent. Sally stood and rubbed Silvio's arm gently. "Maybe you better hear it, Babe. Better to find out now than have it eat you alive."

"It's Zach, isn't it?" Silvio said, a tear running down his cheek. "You and Jeremy DeCiccio. That's why you went after me. You were pregnant. With Zach."

Trysta nodded, her eyes filling again.

"Well, you know what?" Silvio said, the tears now running down his face, "I'm *glad* Jeremy didn't want Zach. Or you. And I'm glad you tricked me into marrying you. That's what you did. Didn't you?"

Trysta nodded, sobbing softly.

"But I'm *glad* you tricked me! Because I'm glad Zach is my son and not his. I'm glad I've got Zach and I'm glad I've got Trina and Sam and Silvia, too. So I don't care about...aw, geeze, Trysta, *Jeremy DeCiccio?* That guy was nothing but a good-looking jerk and everybody knew it. Except you."

"I knew it," Trysta sniffled.

"You knew it? You *knew* it? Then why the heck did you...?" Silvio shook his head.

Trysta stood. "I've got to learn to take care of me before I can take care of anyone else." Then she walked out of Charleston's office.

"Thank you, Mr. Tilley," Laura Cavanni said, heading towards the door while everyone else's eyes followed Trysta. To Silvio she said, "Mr. Jablonski, I'll see you at Zach's appointment next week?"

"Oh...oh, yeah, I guess." Silvio rubbed his hands across his eyes. "Me or my mom will bring him. For his appointment."

"That'll be fine," said Laura.

As Laura Cavanni stepped out of the office Silvio called, "Tell Trysta I said good luck. Finding herself."

Laura turned to him and said with a smile, "I will," then she hurried away to catch up with Trysta.

"You okay, Babe?" Sally said to Silvio.

"Yeah," said Silvio. "As good as you can be after a sucker punch to the gut. But as soon as I get my wind back I'll be fine. Just give me a minute."

"Mr. Jablonski," said Charleston, "you understand that just because Trysta says your son isn't biologically yours doesn't make it true."

"It's probably true," said Silvio.

"Whether it's true or not, in the eyes of the law your son is yours and no one else's."

"That's good to know," said Sally. "Isn't it, Babe?"

"Yeah," said Silvio, "it actually is."

"Anyway, join the club," Darren sighed. "And I don't mean to lay too much on you at once, but in case you want to know who Miri's – Silvia's – father is..."

"What, you know?" said Silvio.

"Yeah."

"Okay," said Silvio, "sure. Tell me."

"In truth this is a good thing to know," said Charleston, "in case God forbid Silvia should exhibit an illness down the road the treatment of which might benefit from knowing her genetic background."

"Right," said Darren. "It's one of the CEO's of Highland and Erskerberg."

"*What?*" cried Sally and Silvio. "Wait," said Silvio, "You're saying that while Trysta was a receptionist at Highland and Erskerberg she was sleeping with a CEO?"

"Well, he *was* a CEO," said Darren. "Jeremy Andrews, the guy who got arrested a couple of months back for fraud. You probably read about it in the news."

"*That guy?*" said Sally. "*That guy* is Silvia's actual father?"

"According to Trysta. When she told him she was pregnant he dumped her. After that she staked me out then pinned me as the father."

"Trysta's trademark move," said Sally.

"Yeah," said Silvio, "she probably had her sights set on that CEO who got her pregnant but when he dumped her she figured you'd be a better catch than I was."

"She had me hooked, all right," said Darren.

"And here she was gay all along," said Sally.

"Hey," said Darren, "you don't think Trysta and Dr. Cavanni are...?"

"*Together?*" Sally finished for him. "What, are you saying Dr. Cavanni could be...*gay?* And dating *Trysta?*"

Darren shrugged. "I don't know about Dr. Cavanni, but I wouldn't put it past Trysta to be gay five minutes before she started seducing women."

"At least with Dr. Cavanni she won't get pregnant," said Sally.

"Trysta being Trysta, I wouldn't put that past her, either," Darren joked.

"But seriously," said Silvio, "I don't care how many women Trysta goes after, and I don't mind if Dr. Cavanni is gay, either, but if she's with Trysta I'm gonna have something to say about taking my son to a psychologist who's dating his mother."

Charleston, who'd been trying to suppress his laughter, said, "I highly doubt that's going on."

"You don't know Trysta," said Darren.

Charleston chuckled, then returned to a more serious tone. "A psychologist who became involved with a patient in that way would be liable to lose her license. My guess would be that Dr. Cavanni was here in the capacity that she alleged: as Trysta's advocate."

"Fine," said Silvio. "She can be that, I guess."

Sally sighed. "Gay or not, I don't think I could just lop off such gorgeous hair."

"She did tell us some things had to happen before she could be herself," said Charleston. "Maybe transforming her appearance was one of those things."

"Yeah," sighed Silvio. "But when I think of how we were married for all those years…how can you be married to someone for so many years and not know them at all?"

Darren and Sally inadvertently met each other's eyes for a moment, then both quickly looked away. Sally blushed and Darren reached into his pocket to glance at his phone. Silvio, suddenly aware of the awkwardness his remark had created, also reddened.

Charleston broke the awkward silence. "Unfortunately it's that very phenomenon that keeps me in business."

"Yeah, I'll bet," said Silvio. "So we're finished, then? We can go?"

"Yes," said Charleston, smiling. "The children are legally in your custody. And you can all go."

"Okay, thanks," said Darren. He hurried out of the office, sniffing and blinking his eyes on his way out.

"Guess he was in a hurry," said Silvio.

"Hey, was he *crying?*" said Sally.

"Looked like it," said Silvio.

Sally pulled in a deep breath. "Wow. All the years I was married to him I never saw him cry. I mean, we had a few knock-down-drag-out yell-fights towards the end of our marriage and even after." She turned to Silvio. "You know what a hot mess of a human volcano I was when you first met me…"

"You and me both back then."

"…but it was always *me* doing all the crying. Never Darren."

Silvio put his arm around Sally. "Maybe he finally sees what he lost."

"And what I found." Sally slipped he arm around Silvio's waist. To Charleston she said, "We can't thank you enough, Mr. Tilley."

"I second that," said Silvio.

"You're both quite welcome," said Charleston. "And may our future meetings always be under equally auspicious circumstances."

After Sally and Silvio had left his office Charleston spent a moment reflecting with gratitude on those occasional cases that served as an affirmation of the path he'd chosen in life.

When Sally and Silvio stepped outside Charleston's office they caught sight of Darren standing down the hall by the elevators. His back was to them, but he appeared to be rubbing his eyes with his sleeve.

"He's still here?" Silvio whispered to Sally.

"Oh, boy," Sally sighed.

"Maybe we should take the stairway?" said Silvio.

"Geeze, we're on the twelfth floor," said Sally.

At that moment Darren turned and saw them. He raised his hand in recognition.

"Too late," Sally sighed, "I guess we're taking the elevator."

When they reached the elevators Darren said, "Hey, you want to call me and we can set up an appointment about your houses?" His eyes looked red but he seemed otherwise himself.

"You bet," said Sally. "We'll give you a call. Real soon."

"We're all going to the lobby, I guess," said Silvio as he pressed the elevator button.

When the elevator door opened Darren stood in front of it, blocking Sally and Silvio's entrance. "Wait," he said, "wait a minute."

"What?" asked Silvio.

"I'm not...I'm not gonna charge you anything to sell your houses."

"What?" cried Sally and Silvio.

"Darren, that's crazy," said Sally.

"Yeah, why wouldn't you charge us to sell our houses?" said Silvio.

"Well, since we're...you know...like family."

Sally and Silvio looked at each other, flummoxed. "Eh, I wouldn't go that far," Silvio muttered.

Darren turned to Silvio. "The kids. Do you think I could...you know, come and see them sometimes? Babysit them and Josh? Maybe take them all out? Out to the mall, to the shore for the day, whatever?"

"You wanna be with my kids?" asked Silvio. "I thought they drove you nuts."

"Well, yeah, they did. But I kinda got used to them, how I used to take care of them, and all. When Trysta wasn't, you know, up to it. Which was actually most of the time. And now I miss them. "

"You *miss* my kids," said Silvio, disbelief in his voice.

"Yeah. And I...I want to be a part of their life."

"Now you do?" said Silvio.

Darren looked down. "Yeah. I want to be a part of their life." He looked back up at Silvio. "And I might as well be, since they're gonna be a part of Josh's life, right?"

"Well, isn't this a flip of the switch," Silvio said to Sally.

"Up to you, Babe," said Sally. "Like he said, he's gonna be around for Josh, anyway."

"Josh, Miri – I mean, Silvia – and little what's-his-name from Mexico, too..."

"His name's David," said Sally, "and he's not from Mexico."

"No?" asked Darren. "Where's he from?"

"He's from Northeast Philly and he's as American as the rest of us. His parents are from Nicaragua."

"Okay, whatever. I'd like to be around for him, too. For all of them. Sometimes." Darren hesitated for a moment then he said, "Silvio, do your kids ever talk about me?"

Silvio sighed. "Yeah, they do sometimes." He considered a moment, then he said, "Yeah, okay, I guess you can see my kids – our kids – sometimes. Be like an uncle, or whatever. I mean, since you did take care of them, and all."

"Thanks, Man," Darren said with a catch in his voice, "that would be great." He cleared his throat then continued, "So how about I swing by your house tonight?"

"*Tonight?*"

"I could, you know, bring a pizza, some ice cream, whatever. Say 'hi' to the kids. Hold Miri for a while. I mean, Silvia. And while I'm there I'll have a look around and we can get the ball rolling on getting the place up for sale." To Sally he said, "If you come over with Josh and...what's his name, again?"

"*David,*" said Sally, "his name's *David.*"

"...Right, David. Anyway, then we could talk about your house, too."

Once again Sally and Silvio stood looking at each other. Sally shrugged.

"Yeah, okay," said Silvio, "since you'll have to come out sometime to look at the house, anyway. Tonight okay with you, Sally?"

"Sure," said Sally. To Darren she said, "Josh always likes going over to Silvio's. And he'll be glad to see you, too."

Darren's face broke into a smile. "Great. It's been too damn quiet in that house in New Conshohocken. I keep thinking I hear somebody knocking on the door. I'm telling you, I can't wait to get out of there."

"You can come around six," said Silvio, "and make sure it's a big pizza."

"Better make that two big pizzas," said Sally, "one pepperoni and one cheese."

"I'll bring three," said Darren, "one pepperoni, one cheese, and one half-and-half."

"Three works," said Silvio.

Then they waited for the elevator, but when it arrived Silvio gestured for Darren to enter. "Me and Sally'll catch the next one," he said.

After Darren disappeared Silvio said, "He's *not* moving in with us."

Sally laughed. "I think he wants to."

"Yeah, he'd like that. For about ten minutes."

"Ten minutes sounds about right. Darren always did have kind of a short interest span." Sally sighed. "Always chasing some dream or another. Dream career, dream house, dream woman."

"He had a dream woman," said Silvio, kissing Sally's cheek.

"No, I mean a fantasy woman. He left his serious college girlfriend for me. Then me for Trysta. Who didn't turn out to be who *she* was pretending to be."

"You can say that again," said Silvio.

"You know," said Sally, "Darren's mother left him when he was, like ten."

"No kidding?" said Silvio.

"Seriously. She just dropped him off one day at his father's house then she drove off in a sporty convertible car with her latest boyfriend. Darren said she was beautiful. Anyway, he ended up being raised by his clueless father and an evil step-mother – who, by the way, always hated me."

"So maybe he's like…looking for his mother?" said Silvio.

"The thought has occurred to me," said Sally.

"Does he have any other family?"

"Nope. Well, except for his gross older step-brother who used to give me the creeps."

"Now I'm kind of feeling sorry for him," said Silvio.

"Yeah, I kind of am, too."

"You think we should let him sell our houses without us paying him?"

Sally laughed. "Hells, yes!"

"Okay, then. I mean, since he wants to be part of our family and all. Between you and me, my kids do actually like him. I don't know why, but they do. So I guess we have room for one more. Even if it is Darren. But he's not moving in."

Sally laughed again. "Silvio," she said, taking his face in her hands, "you're a good, good man. You know that, don't you?"

He put his arms around Sally's waist. "I don't know if I'm a good man or not. But I know I'm a lucky man. And a happy man."

And this time it was a small group of people alighting from a twelfth-floor elevator who were surprised by the sight of two lovers lost in the kind of kiss that only happens in the movies.

ABOUT THE AUTHOR

Patti Liszkay lives in Columbus, Ohio. You can follow her blog at
www.ailantha.com.

NOTE FROM THE AUTHOR

Word-of-mouth is crucial for any author to succeed. If you enjoyed *Hail Mary*, please leave a review online—anywhere you are able. Even if it's just a sentence or two. It would make all the difference and would be very much appreciated.

Thanks!
Patti

Thank you so much for reading one of Patti Liszkay's novels.

If you enjoyed the experience, please check out our recommended for your next great read!

Equal and Opposite Reactions by Patti Liszkay

Set in working-class Northeast Philadelphia and told in urban voices, Equal And Opposite Reactions is a romantic comedy about the chain of events that follows when Sally Miller, a newly divorced, financially struggling young mother and Silvio Jablonski, a broken-hearted plumber who shows up to fix Sally's toilet, learn to their shock that they have something strangely in common.

Their discovery both pulls them into a relationship and leads them down a rabbit hole that causes their lives to become entwined with a constellation of characters including Sally's over-extended, real-estate-managing ex-husband, Silvio's seductive, sexually manipulative ex-wife, a shady South Philadelphia salvage yard operator, a desperate young family of illegal immigrants and a socially-conscious African-American lawyer who becomes their advocate.

But will the volatile chemistry of human emotions bond Sally and Silvio in love, or tear them apart?

www.ingramcontent.com/pod-product-compliance
Lightning Source LLC
Chambersburg PA
CBHW011137100726
47898CB00009B/3012